THE LANTERN

CHARLENE

Enjoy!

Frank

Frank Newell

FRANK NEWELL

This book is a work of fiction. References to real people, events, establishments, organizations, or locales are intended only to provide a sense of authenticity and are used fictitiously. All other characters, and all incidents and dialogue, are drawn from the author's imagination and are not to be construed as real.

ISBN 978-1-945190490

FV- 7P

Published by: Intellect Publishing, LLC
www.IntellectPublishing.com

:

ACKNOWLEDGMENTS

This book would not have been possible without historical details, artifacts, and photographs gathered from the American Heritage Center, University of Wyoming, and clarifying details provided by Pioneer Memorial Museum in Douglas, Wyoming.

Thanks are also due to Phillip Jennings for guidance and recommendations for producing the book and to Jean Gilbertson for editing and research assistance. My partner, Marilyn, was vital to the project for her patience, ongoing support, and excellent proofreading eye.

FRANK NEWELL

DEDICATION

In memory of my father
Walter E. Newell
1889 – 1968

THE LANTERN

*Only those who will risk going too far can possibly find out
how far it is possible to go*
— T.S. Eliot

CHAPTER 1
A YOUNG MAN LAUNCHES HIS DESTINY

March 1913
Pender, Nebraska
The Lindell Hotel

"More coffee, Clint?"

"No thanks, Billy. You made it plenty strong this morning. Anyway, I've got to get ready for work. Big Saturday. It is market day. All the farmers with their spring hogs and cattle will be at the auction. The order buyers who came in yesterday all say demand and prices are up. That means extra cash and a big day for the saloon."

Clint went down the hall to his private room. He put on a starched white shirt, black bow tie, and a black vest. It was a chilly March morning and even though the saloon was just a block up Main Street, he decided to wear his plaid wool jacket and black felt Stetson hat. He picked up the morning *Omaha*

World Herald newspaper as he walked through the lobby out to the unpaved sidewalk and street.

His brisk walk took him past the lumberyard, the feed and grain store, the barbershop, and to the front entrance of Slade's Saloon. Using his master keys, he unlocked the atrium doors. It was just a few steps more to the elegant oak main door on which he used his deadbolt key. As he stepped inside, he relocked the deadbolt and turned on the backbar light. He walked back to his favorite captain's chair at the backbar side table. It was eight a.m. He would have time to read the news before the bar boy returned with the makings of the free lunch, and he had to get the bar ready for opening at nine a.m.

Clint had just turned to the sports page when there was a loud knocking at the door.

"We don't open until nine!"

"Telegram! Telegram, Mr. Clinton."

"All right, Artie. Be right there." Clint unlocked and opened the door.

Artie, the depot boy, handed him the telegram. As Clint started to read the message, Artie said, "You going west, horse trading again this year?"

"Artie, you shouldn't be listening to the incoming telegrams."

"No, sir!"

"I know you do because you watch the depot when John comes for a drink. Well, never mind, Artie. Here is a nickel and be on your way."

Clint was the third son of the six children of Chauncy and Ellen Fisher Morgan. He was favored by his father. His mother came from a prominent, well-to-do Cleveland, Ohio, family. Chauncy also came from a Cleveland family of means. As a youth, he was sent to Harvard. He was to go to law school and then join the family law firm. He dropped out in his third year.

Back home in Cleveland, he met Ellen Fisher. They married in 1880. Financed by Ellen's father, the couple moved to an area soon to be opened for settlement, the Winnebago and Omaha Indian lands of Thurston County, Nebraska.

Chauncy, with his youthful knowledge of horse racing and show horse training, started a successful horse and mule trading business. Sensing the demand for horses and mules in the growing western territories, Chauncy obtained horse and mule contracts from the federal government, the army, and railroads. Financed by his father-in-law, Fred Fisher, he and two partners assembled a herd of more than 200 horses and mules. Early March of 1885, they began their trek west from Omaha to Wyoming, Montana, and Canada, trading, buying, and selling. Home by early October, after their last sale, they divided a $5,000 profit. That established the Chauncy Morgan Horse and Mule Trading Company and the annual trading trip west.

In the twenty-five years after the opening of the Omaha and Winnebago lands for homesteading and Indian land leasing by the federal government, Pender had become a community of well-to-do families. Daughters of farm families were hired by the more affluent to be maids, cooks, and nannies. Sons and daughters of the well-to-do were sent to the University of Nebraska. Many of the daughters were sent to music conservatories; others, to finishing schools.

The social life of the young unmarried was full: lively church socials, traveling live theater at the Opera House, picnics, and walks and buggy rides.

Clint's best friend, Wesley Lowe, introduced him to his sister, Carrie, who was the housemaid and cook for the Nye family. At the age of twenty-three, Clint was far from ready to settle down, but he liked Carrie. They dated often and soon became quite fond of each other. They took long evening walks through the city park. They sat together on a picnic table bench, sharing their dream of having their own farm in the lush Logan Valley. It was their hope that as savings from their jobs grew, they would find a way to make the dream come true.

Then there was Marie Mahoney. Marie was the daughter of Jim Mahoney, a wealthy land investor and commercial building contractor. Just nineteen, she was a petite, radiantly beautiful, auburn-haired free spirit—often to the total consternation of her mother. Her sister, Mary, twenty-six, was a talented pianist who had just earned her PhD in music and accepted a professorship at a small, prestigious Oregon university. But Marie, like Clint, was far from ready to settle down.

A grand social event was the annual round-trip Train Excursion to Sioux City. Young couples boarded the early afternoon train (with chaperones) arriving in time for some downtown shopping, then off to the Sioux Ballroom for a dinner dance. The chaperones made sure everyone made it to the depot to board the last train south to Pender.

The 1912 Train Excursion was set for March 10. Clint had the night off and planned to take Carrie, but Carrie had to prepare a special Nye family dinner and couldn't get away. Without a second thought, Clint asked Marie, and she said, "Yes! I'm so excited!" She had always liked Clint and just knew they were going to have a great time.

Well, they did—so much so they missed the train. Marie sent a wire to her mother saying that they would be at her cousin Effie's home for the night and be home in the morning. They took a cab to Cousin Effie's. Effie pointed out to them two upstairs bedrooms. It was cold, so they just climbed into the double bed of the first room. Effie's mom later checked on them and saw them in one bed. She didn't say a word, but the next morning, she handed Marie an envelope to give to her mother. After she got home, Marie innocently gave the letter to her mother. The next day Marie was at the depot with her luggage, thirty dollars, and a ticket to Salem, Oregon, to be with her sister.

Carrie picked up on the gossip and, in a pique, accepted the proposal of a young German whom she had dated before Clint.

With both Marie and Carrie gone, life in Pender over the next year was a lot duller for Clint. *Maybe I should just go on the Trek and get out of here for a while.* But he also had reason not to sign on for the 1913 Horse and Mule Trading Trek West with his father. This would be his tenth year of the Trek West—if he went. Without thinking about it, he rubbed at the two-inch scar on his cheek, his constant reminder of the vow he had made the previous year never to go on the Trek again.

Clint had dropped out of high school in 1904 at the age of fifteen and joined his father, soon becoming a top hand on the annual Horse and Mule Trading Trek West. He had stayed with it every year since. In the off-season, he worked as a bar boy in Slade's Saloon.

But this year's Trek? Clint pushed his hands through his hair. *Might as well open the telegram.* Walking to his chair, he sat back and slowly read the wire: "Leaving Monday a.m. from St. Louis. 20 car train fine horses and mules. As usual we will sell and trade west and north to Canada. Home by Oct. Big bonus. St. Louis ticket $20 money order at depot Sunday a.m. Your father, Chauncy."

Clint folded the telegram and put it into his back pocket. Clearly his father was expecting him. As he finished getting the backbar setups ready, the owner, Jim Slade, and the bar boy came in from the back door.

"Good morning, Clint," said Jim. "Are we ready to open?"

Slade's Saloon was up to date in every respect: electric lights, sanitary flush toilets and urinals, backbar with hot and cold running water, iced beer on tap. Mud or manure boots were not allowed on the polished oak floor.

As Clint got ready for the early customers (businessmen fresh from a shave at the next-door barbershop), he pondered over the telegram. *I really meant that vow! I swore I would never go again after last year.* Then he saw it all again in his mind: Coming back to Sheridan after delivery of two saddle ponies, he had been attacked by three renegade Sioux Indians. In the melee, they had stolen his $200 in gold and his horse, and left him on foot with an ugly knife wound on his left cheek. He had rejoined the crew, dead tired, after a long night's walk back to Sheridan. Doc Graves, the vet, had treated the cut on his cheek.

By late October, when all the stock was sold and the trading was over for the year, they boarded the train bound for home to Nebraska. Chauncy divided up the bonuses. It had been a good year. Clint thought he would get $500, same as the rest. Chauncy instead gave Clint $300 to make up for the $200 his son had lost to the renegades.

He was still thinking about his vow just before the nine a.m. opening. He showed the saloon owner the telegram.

"Jim, I swore I would never go again after what happened last time. But there is nothing here for me, now that both Marie and Carrie are gone."

"Clint, I understand. You got some mixed feelings about it, but I reckon you will be leaving early in the morning. But finish the day here. I owe you twenty dollars for this week. Then you got to pack. And if we don't have time for a word this evening, good luck, and I'll see you in October."

The bar and tables were full soon after the opening hour. Clint never stopped: tending the bar, meeting and greeting new and old friends, but never said a word to anyone about his leaving—until, around four, when his special friend, Duncan Laird, came in and up to the bar.

"Greetings, my boy." Duncan, a tall, bony, Scot farmer, held an unusual bond of friendship with Clint, probably because the younger man was always willing to listen to Duncan, after a few Scotches, recite Bobby Burns poetry. It was one of the few times Clint indulged his deep interest in words and language, and he loved a good turn of phrase. They shared a Scotch. "Ye going west this year, Clint, me boy?"

"Yes, Duncan. Looks like I am. Leaving in the morning."

"Be safe this time, save your money, and you have a job on my farm when you get home in October."

"Thanks, Duncan. See you in October."

Duncan turned back to his Scotch, took a sip, and launched into a few lines of Robert Burns poetry, which Clint paused to hear:

> But, Mousie, thou art no thy lane,
> In proving foresight may be vain:
> The best laid schemes o' mice an' men
> Gang aft a-gley,
> An' lea'e us nought but grief an' pain
> For promised joy.

Clint left early. Back in the Lindell Hotel, he enjoyed a late supper of beef stew. Mrs. Smith came out of the kitchen and sat with Clint. "Bessie, I'm leaving in the morning," Clint said. "Going on the usual Horse and Mule Trek West. Hope it is my last."

"Yes, I know. Jim told me."

"Keep my room for me, Bessie. I'll be back in October."

Early Sunday morning, Clint put on his wool shirt, jeans, and Lucchese boots. In his valise, he packed his personals, a change of clothes, and his .38 with holster and belt. He picked up his battered, cloth-covered copy of Ralph Waldo Emerson's

15

essay *Self-Reliance* and thumbed through the pages, reading again his favorite lines, most especially, *Trust thyself: every heart vibrates to that iron string.* He breathed in deeply, feeling that iron string taut within himself. The thin book also went into the bag. Next he put on his wool Pendleton jacket and black Stetson hat. He had a quick cup of coffee and a donut. Out the side door of the hotel, he made it to the depot just in time. Artie had his ticket to St. Louis and twenty dollars, and handed it to him just as the train was steaming out.

Clint boarded the passenger car. He was alone. He sat relaxed across two seats and put his boots on the seat in front of him. Pushing his hat over his eyes, he gave in to the rhythm of the train and napped the two-hour trip to Omaha.

At the Omaha depot, he boarded the southbound train to St. Louis. There were few passengers. He found one of the reclining chair seats, stashed his valise under the seat, and proceeded to the dining car. The porter handed him a copy of the Sunday *World Herald.* He ordered the steak sandwich lunch, apple pie, and coffee.

As he ate, he tried reading the newspaper, but his mind drifted to thoughts of home and Carrie and Marie. He sighed deeply with the emptiness in his heart. *I don't even know where they are—either one of them. Carrie is somewhere with another man as her husband when it really should be me. And Marie— who ever knows where Marie is! Will I ever see them again? Does it even make sense to go back to Pender after this Trek? I wouldn't be going back to either one of them, so what's in Pender for me?* He told himself that maybe on this Trek he would find a new land of opportunity.

In an effort to shake off his unhappiness, he began to think about his younger brother, who, unlike Clint, had stayed in school and graduated, and then went on to the University of Nebraska. He was a senior now with big plans to continue with

16

his education and become a professor in English literature at the university. He shared Clint's love of words and reading and writing and he was making his dream a reality. As the train rocked him back and forth, Clint began to daydream that perhaps he could yet finish up his high school education and then go on to the university, the same as his brother had done. Of course, his true ambition had always been to have a farm of his own in the valley. *Is there any way I could do both?* He dug into his valise for the Emerson essay and focused his attention on the philosophy that had always given him strength.

> *Man is his own star; and the soul that can*
> *Render an honest and a perfect man,*
> *Commands all light, all influence, all fate…*

The day passed quickly. As the reality of joining Chauncy and the work crew approached, Clint arranged with the conductor for a stop at the stockyards depot. At eleven p.m., the train slowed coming into the stockyards and stopped at the small platform. Clint got off as the train moved on to the St. Louis terminal. He peered through the darkness across the tracks, where he saw the flickering lights of a Pullman car and knew it must be Chauncy's. Cutting across three sets of tracks, he got to the Pullman car door. He stepped up and in. There was Chauncy at his desk. "Welcome, Son. You're just in time. We leave in one hour. You will bunk with Doc Graves. His car is next to the cook and crew car. You, like always, will help Doc and be in charge of the work crew.

"Our first stop is Dodge City. We will be there in about two days. Bill, my advance man, is already there getting ads in the papers and posting bills announcing our arrival. Best horses and mules ever. Sale prices are up. Big bonus! See you later, Son."

Doc Graves was in his bunk. Clint tried not to wake him, but he heard him getting settled in. "Well, hello, Clint. Good to have you on board again. Looks like we will have a fine trek."

"I hope so, Doc," Clint said.

Doc Graves was one of the best equine veterinarians in the country—as long as he was sober. One of Clint's responsibilities was to keep him off the stuff. Not only did Doc have to keep the traveling herd disease-free, every sale and trade must be examined by Doc and be given his certified bill of health.

The work crew, one in each car with the animals, were experienced and reliable. Clint supervised the loading/unloading of hay, grain, and clean water. The first leg of the trip to Dodge City was uneventful. Sales and trades were brisk. At the end of two days, Chauncy had added an excellent $3,000 profit after expenses.

Clint's work for this leg of the Trek was done. Since Doc Graves was sound asleep in his bunk, Clint read again the vaudeville ad in the paper and decided he might as well take in the show. The Opera House was several blocks uptown. He was late and missed the opening acts. There were a couple of seats down front, so he got to sit near the stage. The acrobatic team of The von Essens, Fredrik and Hans, had just ended. Next up was the featured performance of Miss Lily Longine. Lily came on stage, moving slowly to the center stage piano. She was tall, lithe, and absolutely stunning in a full-length, beaded white gown. As he sat down, she turned to the audience. At that instant, she and Clint caught each other's eye. "My God," Clint said under his breath. "It's Marie!"

Clint sat mesmerized, his brain transfixed, but he noticed that Marie often looked directly at him. Near the end of her performance, the stage lights dimmed. Clint quietly rose from his aisle seat and walked up and around to the side exit. It had been a full year since he had seen Marie, but he intended to see her now. He walked down the alley to the stage door. He waited a few minutes, then entered (there was no one at the entrance) and went down the hall to her dressing room. As he neared her door, he heard a muffled German voice and Marie screaming, "Nein! No!" He opened the door. It was Fredrik, the acrobat, mauling her.

"Get out!" Clint said, in a firm, tough voice.

"Who are you?" Fredrik replied.

Clint repeated, "Unhand her and leave!"

With that, Fredrik turned and pulled a derringer from his pocket and fired, hitting Clint in his left shoulder.

Clint reached for his .38 and shot Fredrik right through his left chest. Fredrik doubled up and fell across a chair.

On stage, the band was playing with very loud drum riffs to a dog and pony act. No one heard the gunshots.

"Marie, we've got to get out of Dodge. Change to a traveling dress and shoes. I'll help you pack one bag." In ten minutes, they were out the stage door, down the alley, and back on the street towards the stockyards and train depot.

On the way, Clint asked, "Marie, do you have any money?"

"Just five dollars," she replied. "They didn't pay me."

"Here's thirty dollars. At the depot, get a twenty-five-dollar ticket for as far west as you can go—west to your sister in Oregon, if possible. I will wait around the corner of the depot. The midnight train is coming in."

Marie came out of the depot with her ticket. The porter helped her with her bag. She waved to Clint as she boarded.

Clint ran down to the stockyards, grabbed a fast horse he knew, and saddled up. In a fast gallop, he left Dodge, going north. The derringer bullet had grazed his shoulder. There wasn't much bleeding, but he knew he had to get to a doctor to clean the wound.

Riding fast, he wasn't sure if his .38 had killed the German. He assumed the man lay dead in Marie's dressing room and would be found within the hour.

As Clint would later learn, the dead Fredrik was found within thirty minutes by his brother Hans, who had been waiting in the brothers' dressing room. Their plan was to have dinner together, as they always did after a show. Instead, when Hans went looking for Fredrik, he found him slumped over a chair in Marie's dressing room, in a pool of blood, and Marie nowhere in sight. *Could Marie have...?* Hans was too stunned to finish the thought. He went to the only friend he knew, the Opera House stage manager, who called the Sheriff. But it was too late for Fredrik. The only place to take him was the funeral home. Only half listening to the coroner, Hans made plans for a casket and a return trip to Germany to bury his brother in the family cemetery.

After four hours of hard riding, Clint, exhausted, stopped to rest. Dawn was breaking and he saw lights a mile or so ahead. He walked towards the lights and came to the main business block. At the front door of the corner brick building hung a small sign: "Sam Johnson, M.D." Clint tethered his horse to the hitching post, walked to the door, and knocked.

Just as Clint started to knock again, the door opened. A slightly stooped man peered over his glasses at Clint.

"Dr. Johnson?"

"Yes. Come in." The doctor saw Clint's blood-soaked shirt. As he helped Clint take off his shirt, he said, "What happened?"

"Took a bullet. Could have been worse, I guess."

"No need to tell me more, Son. Sit over here by the table."

The doctor left the room for a few minutes, then returned from the kitchen with a pan of hot water, towel, soap, and iodine. As he washed off the caked blood, he saw where the bullet had grazed Clint's shoulder, no more than a half-inch deep. "Good. No bullet fragments." He applied iodine and carefully stitched the six-inch gash closed.

Dr. Johnson took a bottle of whiskey from his medicine cabinet and set it on the table. "This will help ease the pain," he said, as he poured a large shot glass full and handed it to Clint.

Clint downed the whiskey and cleared his throat. "Thanks, Doc."

"And I don't reckon you have any more use for this." Dr. Johnson grabbed Clint's shirt and wadded the blood-soaked half inside. "I'll see if I don't have a clean shirt for you upstairs. And I got some coffee brewing. Be back in a minute with a cup."

He returned with a work shirt that had seen a lot of use, but, as promised, it was clean and the size wasn't too far off. In his other hand was a cup of black coffee..

"You can chase that whiskey with this," the doctor said, handing Clint the coffee. "You're exhausted, Son, and your horse is winded. The livery stable is just around the block. Miss Harriet's Boarding House is in the next block. Get some breakfast and rest. Where are you headed?"

"I don't rightly know," said Clint. "They're looking for roustabouts in the oil patch east of here. Might try that. Thanks Doc, for the coffee and the whiskey and…" He pointed toward his stitched shoulder.

"That will be four dollars," said Doc. Clint gave him his last five, and the doctor dug in his pocket and handed him a dollar. "Good luck, Son."

Chauncy heard a hard knock on his Pullman car side door. He looked up from his desk and peered out the window. It was

21

Sheriff Billy Christian and two of his deputies. "Billy, come in," Chauncy said.

"Chauncy, how you been? Missed seeing you last year," said Billy.

Chauncy and Billy were friends from the old days, herding the horses and mules across the prairie west from town to town. "How's the family, Billy?"

"All growed up. Wife's fine."

"What can I do for you, Billy? We're movin' out in about an hour," said Chauncy.

"There was a shooting over at the Opera House sometime last night."

"Yeah, I heard," said Chauncy.

"One of them German acrobat boys was found in Lily Longine's dressing room. You remember her?"

"Sure do."

"Anyway, that German fella was found dead, shot right through the left chest with a .38. Looked like she left in a hurry. We think on the midnight train. The dead German had a derringer in his right hand. We are just looking through the yards here. Your boys all on board?"

"Yup," said Chauncy. "Well, you never know about them traveling vaudeville show people. Probably one of them got jealous of Lily Longine. Maybe a lovers' quarrel—something like that."

Billy nodded, as though he was considering that. "Well, Chauncy. We'll be on our way. See you next year?"

"I'll be here, same time," said Chauncy.

Clint hadn't checked in, and now Chauncy knew why. Only Clint carried a .38.

They moved on to the next stops. Chauncy always thought Clint would show up along the way. But he never did.

Trouble creates a capacity to handle it
— Oliver Wendell Holmes

CHAPTER 2
DESTINY OFF COURSE

At the livery stable, Clint got the saddle off the tired pony.

"That's a fine little bay mare you got there. Ever think about selling her?" said the liveryman.

"Matter of fact, I have," said Clint. "What is your offer?"

"Well, best I could do is about thirty-five."

"Pony and saddle, fifty-five," said Clint.

"Done," said the liveryman. "Come in my office. I'll get a bill of sale and the cash." Inside, he eyed Clint and asked, "What did you say your name was?"

"Barnes. Jim Barnes," said Clint.

"All right. Here you are," as he counted out five tens and a five.

Cash in hand, Clint walked up the street to Harriet's Boarding House and Café. There he ordered breakfast of bacon, eggs, hash browns, and coffee. As he ate, he thought about where to go. He considered working in the wheat harvest in the west. But the early harvest wouldn't start for at least six weeks, and he had to keep moving on. A job in the oil fields east was

23

his only choice. As he paid for his breakfast, he asked Harriet about ways to get to the oil patch.

"There is an eastbound stage in about an hour, or you might see if you could get a ride on one of the freight wagons."

Clint made it to the station just as the eastbound Butterfield stage was ready to leave. He paid the agent twenty dollars for a ride to El Dorado. Six young roustabouts were crowded into the cabin. The driver invited Clint to ride shotgun. He jumped up to the right seat. The driver grabbed the reins and with a "Hi!" and a crack of his short whip to the four-horse team, they were off.

The day went well. After about an hour rolling east on the El Dorado trail, the driver handed the reins to Clint. "Take 'em," he said. "I need a drink." He reached down to the side boot and pulled out a pint, took a long drag, and handed it to Clint as he took back the reins. Clint declined and shoved the bottle in the right boot.

"You handle them pretty good, Son," the driver said. "Where did you learn?"

"From my dad," Clint replied.

At the twenty-mile post, they pulled into the remount station. "All right, boys," the driver shouted. "Thirty minutes! Chow and coffee inside." A quick meal of beans, cornbread, apple pie, and hot black coffee. Then a trip to the outhouse or a piss by the water tank. With a fresh team, the driver yelled, "Let's go! El Dorado by dark."

"Hell, El Dorado is the driest of the dry," said one of the roustabouts, his voice heavy with disgust and disappointment.

"Not if you know what I know," said another.

"What do you know?"

The young fella chuckled. "I know a place a guy can get as much whiskey as his stomach can hold. The real stuff."

"Well, tell us!"

The young man leaned back, enjoying his privileged information. "You know, I can't rightly give you an address, or anything like that, but I can let you follow me for a dollar."

"A dollar!"

"A dollar each."

A chorus of complaints came from the roustabouts, but everyone knew they would all find a dollar when they reached El Dorado.

With the whiskey to look forward to, the stagecoach passengers passed the trip more easily. It didn't seem long at all before the driver braked to a stop. "Whoa!" he said to the team. "Here she is, boys." Everyone stepped out in front of the El Dorado Hotel. Five roustabouts already had a dollar each at the ready, and they set off following the sixth toward the backroom saloon. Clint hadn't paid a dollar to the young fella. He helped Buck unhitch the team. "Thanks," said Buck. "See you again sometime."

Clint went in the hotel entrance. "How much for a room?"

"Two dollars. Three, with a bath," the desk clerk said.

"I'll take it," Clint replied.

The clerk handed him the key to Room 3, next to the bath. As Clint walked up the carpeted stairs to the room, he thought about Marie and wondered if she had made it to Salem and her sister. He was exhausted. It seemed like a bad lifetime dream, all that had happened to him. Though he was only one day from Dodge City, he felt safe. Tomorrow he would try for a job in the oil patch.

Marie never made it to Portland/Salem, Oregon, to her sister. That night in the lounge car she met a handsome young man who introduced himself by saying he was a talent agent. Over drinks, he persuaded her to go with him to Los Angeles. He said he would introduce her to motion picture producers and directors,

25

and help her get jobs performing in the best Los Angeles nightclubs.

She never made stardom, but gradually drifted away, her identity and whereabouts lost to friends and family.

In the bathroom of the El Dorado Hotel, Clint took off the doctor's work shirt, shaking out the stagecoach dust. He carefully removed Doc Johnson's bandage. The bullet wound was healing and there was no infection. Doc had done well. He washed up and dressed. The hotel clerk provided directions to the saloon, and Clint headed there at once.

Off in a corner of the saloon he saw the six roustabouts, but their heads were together over the table and they didn't notice him. He found a place at the end of the bar. "Whiskey."

The bartender, a tall, burly, friendly sort, set up a full bottle and shot glass. As Clint poured his first shot, the man next to him said, looking down, "Pretty fancy boots there. Lucchese?"

"Yup," replied Clint.

"Don't see many of them around here, except on some of the oil bosses."

Clint never answered. He downed a second shot, dropped a dollar on the bar, and headed out the door and back to the hotel, bound for the dining room. He ordered the rib steak dinner, fresh bread, strawberry jam, and hot, black coffee. The dinner was good, just seventy-five cents. He tipped the waiter twenty-five cents and asked, "Where are they hiring for the oilfield?"

"Hiring hall is two blocks down. Better get there early. They open six a.m., and there is always a lineup."

"Thanks," Clint said.

Clint locked the door to his room. At the window, he peered to the street below and noted the back stairwell. He opened the window for fresh air. He sat in the chair by the bed and pulled off his boots. He laid his pants and shirt over the chair back and, socks off, climbed into bed, his .38 by his side. He dozed into a restless sleep. As he turned to his right side, his chair fell to the floor. He sat up and saw, reflected in the moonlight in front of the window, a man holding his boots—the same man who at the bar had admired them. Clint pointed his .38 at the man and said, "Drop my boots, boy, or you will not only be bootless and barefoot but under six feet on Boot Hill!" The boots hit the floor and the man was out the window and down the backstairs. Clint closed the window, sat down on the bed, and said to himself: "This damn place isn't as safe as I thought!"

At five-thirty that morning, Clint was at the hiring hall, third man in line. The clerk looked up at him. "Name?"

"Bill Smith," said Clint.

"What can you do?"

"I'm good with horses and mules."

"You are hired. Five dollars a day, with lunch. Freight wagons leave here at seven. You will go to Standard Oil Field 1. Next door, get steel-toe boots, horsehide gloves, and overalls."

Clint changed into his work outfit and took his clothes back to the hotel. For twenty-five cents, the desk clerk found a valise for him and hid his boots in the locked closet.

The wagon driver let him off at the foreman's shack. Out with ten other men, he found himself lifting iron and steel rigging. There were no horses or mules. After three days of back-breaking labor, he could take no more. After turning in the shoes, gloves, and overalls for credit, he left with just five dollars.

Now nearly broke, Clint wandered down to the livery stable, inquiring about work.

"I haven't anything," came the reply. "Wait. You said you knew horses and mules? There is a custom wheat harvest outfit about ready to leave. They're down at the stockyards. Might try them."

At the railroad track siding, he found the harvest manager's freight car. Inside the car, he introduced himself: "Bill Smith."

"Sam Harmon. What can I do for you?"

"Mr. Harmon, I'm very good at handling horses and mules. Could you use a good hand? I need a job. I am single and can move with your outfit."

"What is your experience?" asked Harmon.

"Five years with the Chauncy Morgan Trading Company."

"I've heard of them. Good, honest traders. We need a good man. Pay is twenty-five dollars a month plus keep. We move out tomorrow, traveling west through the harvest. Finish up in Nebraska by September."

As they shook hands, Harmon said, "You can bunk in the foreman's car."

"I'll go up to the hotel and check out."

"Good. I'll tell Tom Shaw to expect you."

Clint joined the wheat harvest work crew. They moved farm to farm, south, west, and north to western Nebraska. As time went on that spring and summer, he thought often of Marie and wondered if he would ever see her again. And of Carrie, now married and lost forever. While he wasn't sure it was safe to go home, he hoped that by September he would make it to Wyoming and find Chauncy.

After a summer of farm work, travel, vaudeville shows, and gambling (poker), Clint was nearly broke. In Sidney, Nebraska, the first of October, he checked into the Sidney Hotel and Saloon. With his last twenty-five dollars, he decided to go down to the saloon, have a few drinks, and find a poker game. "Is there a game on tonight?" he asked the bartender.

"Should be starting soon, back room," the bartender said.

"Thanks," Clint said, as he walked down the hall to the side door. As he entered the room, he said, "Gentlemen, may I join you?"

"One chair open," said the dealer.

Clint sat down, introducing himself as Bill Smith.

"Five-card stud. Ante," the dealer said.

Clint stayed in for about an hour. He was not doing well and soon learned the game was too rich for him. After eleven-thirty he said, "Fellas, I'm near broke. Check me out."

"You're out. Better luck next time."

He had just enough money for a drink and a couple of dollars to spare after that. He was sitting hunched over his one drink, feeling as miserable and lonely and broke as he had ever felt in his life, when he began to overhear a conversation at a table behind him. "That vaudeville show is coming to Denver and I hear it's really something," said one man.

Another man answered, "I heard down in Dodge City the star of the show got involved in a murder and nobody knows what happened but she left. But here's the thing: after the performance somebody saw a man leave by the side door wearing a black Stetson and a pair of real fancy boots. Folks there are thinking he might have had something to do with the murder of the acrobat."

Suddenly Clint's mind was razor sharp. He glanced down to make sure he didn't have his handmade Lucchese boots on. No, he was wearing his Wolverine work shoes, dirty jeans, and a work shirt. His fine black Stetson and the boots were stored in the valise. As casually as he could manage, Clint stood and sauntered out of the saloon. He retrieved his valise and took it back behind the building to a burn barrel, which fortunately was out of the moonlight in the shadow of the building. He stuffed some newspaper into the barrel, then his fine Stetson and his beautiful Lucchese boots, then more newspaper before lighting a fire. He stayed long enough to see the hat consumed and the boots crisped beyond recognition. His .38 was in the valise too, but that he kept.

Dead tired now and utterly dispirited, Clint went up to his room, turned in, and hoped that tomorrow would be a better day.

Mid-morning he checked out of the hotel and had breakfast. It was a clear, early-autumn day.

Leaving the hotel, Clint headed for the Union Pacific depot three blocks away. As he got to the depot, he realized that his last dollar was not going to buy him a ticket to anywhere.

Just before the depot, he saw a slow-moving freight, southbound to Denver. He ran across the passenger northbound tracks. Running alongside the freight, he grabbed the side bar of an open, empty boxcar. In the boxcar were two other men in one corner, leaning on a bale of hay. Clint moved to the other end, where he could keep an eye on them. He was desperate and despondent. He had never ridden the rails. He thought that when he got to Denver, he could find work and eventually get home to Pender.

Though it was a fast-moving freight, the miles seemed to pass on forever. Mid-afternoon he fell asleep.

Clint awoke with a start, his head throbbing. He felt in his pockets. Gone were his .38 and the last dollar. The only thing left by the thieves was his old cloth-covered copy of *Self-Reliance*. He peered out the open boxcar. To his right was a depot sign: Cheyenne! It was early morning, the day after he left Sidney. The train was rolling out of Cheyenne to Douglas. He was shivering from the dry cold morning. He had been beaten and robbed. He had nothing to eat but a small cheese sandwich from the Sidney Hotel. Hungry and forlorn, he rode on.

About three p.m., the freight came into Douglas. Clint got off. He knew the town from his past trips through with Chauncy.

A chill northwest wind was gusting dust through the street. He walked two blocks to the nearest saloon. As he walked in, he felt the warmth of the coal stove, back at the end of the bar. He found a chair and sat close to the stove. No one said a word and he felt safe. A few minutes later, a tall, burly, gruff-voiced man came in, turned to the bar, and said, "I'm in need of a ranch hand. Seen anybody looking for work?"

Without a word, the bartender pointed to Clint.

Striding up to Clint, he said, "Son, you ever done any range riding?"

Clint looked up and replied, "Yes, sir."

"Wait a minute. You look like one of Chauncy Morgan's boys. What happened to you? Never mind. I'm Jim Brown, foreman/manager of Careyhurst, the CY brand. I've got forty head of polled Hereford heifers just in from Texas. We have to herd them to the main ranch, and I need another hand. Want the job?"

"Yes, sir," said Clint.

"Good. Need to get you cleaned up and outfitted. Pay is thirty dollars a month and keep. Here's some chits. First, go up the street to the general store. Give them a chit and they will fix you up. Then go across the street to the bath and barber shop. Give the barber a chit. Get yourself a bath and shave. Then next door is a good restaurant. Use your last chit. You look like you haven't had a square meal in a while. All is charged to half your first two months' pay. After you eat, go on down to the stockyards barn. You can sleep there tonight. The hands will know you're coming. They will fix you up with your horse and saddle. We move out six a.m."

Clint rose up from his chair. He and Brown shared a hearty shake of hands. Clint said, "Thank you. I'll be there."

"You come from a good family. Do well and you have a job for the winter," said Brown.

31

Chits in hand, Clint made his first stop, the general store. He kept thinking: *Is this really true?* He gave the chit to the clerk. "Got a job with Careyhurst."

"They are tough, but they are the best," he said. "Come with me. Looks like you are going to need everything."

A half hour later, Clint had a complete outfit: work boots, socks, long johns, boot-cut jeans, belt, shirts, neckerchief, Stetson, winter earmuff cap, leather gloves, wool jacket, personal hygiene kit, knife, and bedroll. Packages in hand, he walked across the street to the barber shop. Inside, he put everything in a chair and gave his barber chit to the front man.

"Okay. One of Brown's men. Come on back for a bath. Think you need one," he said.

After the bath he dressed in his new clothes. After the haircut and shave, he was ready for a meal. It was six p.m. At the Douglas Dinner House next door, he left his bedroll and package with the hostess. He gave her his last chit. She nodded and showed him to a window table. "Enjoy," she said. Famished, he ordered the rib eye steak dinner with his favorite, fresh bread, jam, and hot coffee—his first meal in two days.

The mantel clock struck seven p.m. as he left the restaurant. Making his way through the Burlington railyards, he saw the empty boxcar he had left just four hours ago. Now he had a job, cowboy with the CY brand. He would be riding through the Platte River Valley, much of the same areas he rode in years past when he was with Chauncy, delivering horses and mules.

Though it was early evening, it was pitch dark. As Clint walked down the road to the stockyards, he came upon lighted lanterns hanging from high posts. The path of the lanterns through the corrals led him to the side door of the barn. Inside, he was met by Jim Brown.

"Clint, looks like you're all fixed up. Have a good dinner?" asked Brown.

"Yes, sir. Thank you," said Clint.

"C'mon, meet the men you will be riding with. Boys, meet Clint Morgan. He is a good horseman, worked for the Chauncy Traders and knows this country," said Brown.

Clint shook hands with each of the four men.

"Like to join our poker game?"

"No, thanks," said Clint. "If you don't mind, I've got to turn in. Haven't slept much in two days."

He found two open bales of hay, laid out his bedroll, took off his boots and jacket, covered, and was soon sound asleep. In no time at all, he heard Jim say, "Rise and shine. It's five. We leave at daybreak."

At the cook shack next door, they had a hearty breakfast of bacon, eggs, biscuits, gravy, and hot coffee. Out in the horse corral, they saddled up. Frank McDuffie helped Clint bridle and saddle a fine young bay mare.

As dawn broke, the cattle corral gate was opened. The Herefords had been fed and watered, and were ready to go. Each cowboy took his turn carefully moving the herd through the gate, down the road. At the edge of town, they turned the herd off the road towards the river.

By ten a.m., they were moving northwest across the Platte Valley. As far as the eye could see, the knee-high, bluestem grass waved in the breeze, glistening in the sun. Pronghorn antelope scattered just ahead, their horns and heads bobbing through grass. At noon, they stopped at a watering pond fed by a small stream. They watered the cattle and horses, rested, and had a lunch of hard-roll meat sandwiches and hot coffee.

Brown cut ten of the Herefords from the herd. He had Billy and his three boys take them to the north ranch. Brown, Frank, and Clint went on to Careyhurst with the remaining thirty. They reached the first fenced pastures at dusk and were soon at the cattle corrals. Ranch hands opened the gate to the Herefords corral. Brown, Frank, and Clint rode on past the pastures filled with brood cows and yearlings, on up the rise to the horse corrals, barns, foreman/manager's home, owner's mansion, and cowboy quarters.

This was Careyhurst, heart of a ranch of owned and federal-lease lands on both sides of the North Platte River from Douglas to Casper. Joseph Maull Carey had, over the previous decades, put together owned lands of about six thousand acres with some fifty thousand acres leased from the federal government for grazing.

Now, as Brown, Frank, and Clint reached the main horse corral, they turned their horses over to the ranch hands.

"Good ride, Clint. Frank, get Clint settled in," Brown said, as he walked to his manager's house.

Across the road was a long, white, brick building, with smoke and steam coming out of two chimneys. "This is the bath and cookhouse," Frank said. The bathhouse was equipped with both hot and cold running water, as was the cookhouse, where the men ate their meals. Just above on a knoll was a row of attached one-room apartments. "Number 6 is vacant. You can bunk there next to mine. Drop your gear inside and we will go down and get some chow," said Frank.

Clint dropped his saddlebags on the single bed and sat on the edge of the bed. He was dog-tired. The room had a small coal-burning stove, table, two chairs, and a kerosene lamp. First class for the best cowboys. When Frank came by, they walked down to the cookhouse, stopping first at the washroom. With warm water, soap, and a clean towel, Clint washed the trail dust from his face and hands.

At a cookhouse table, they joined two young cowboys and were soon served a hearty meal of roast beef with all the fixings, topped off with apple pie and cups of strong, hot coffee.

"Clint, I hear you are a pretty fair horseman," Frank said.

"I've had a fair bit of time working with horses and mules," Clint said.

"You will do fine here," said Frank. "Been with the Careys five years now, saving to get my own spread someday soon. There is homestead land opening up near Glenrock and Casper."

Then Clint heard a sound that surprised him: the sound of children laughing, running, playing. "What's that? Kids here?"

Frank nodded. "Lots of the men have their families here with them, so there are lots of kids. Down toward the river is housing for the families, and there's a one-room school on the creek where the kids spend the day. There's also a country store where the wives do their shopping."

"A store – here?"

"Yes. When that Chicago and Northwestern Railroad train comes in to the Careyhurst station, it always has supplies to restock the store. You can find most anything you need there, all sorts of groceries, fuel, some machinery, and things the wives like for the house. And the Post Office is run out of there too, in case you want to mail something."

Frank walked with Clint past the cluster of buildings where the train stopped: along with the store and a depot, there was a section house, a big machinery warehouse, stockyards, and a lumberyard. Clint shook his head as the immensity of Careyhurst began to dawn on him. But it had been a long day and he was tired. "Frank, I think I'll turn in. I want to be rested and ready for tomorrow, my first day."

"See you at breakfast," said Frank.

Clint sat on the bed, took his boots off, and lay down. In wonder of it all, he tried to put out of his mind that dreadful night at the Dodge City Opera House. He hoped Marie had made it to her sister in Oregon. But most of all, he wanted to be home. In his heart, he knew that someday, no matter what he had done to lose her, Carrie, the only woman he had ever loved, would be with him forever.

As with people, so with places: love is unforeseen…
— Muriel Spark

CHAPTER 3
SETTLING IN AS CAREYHURST EQUINE MANAGER

Clint was up early. Before breakfast, he walked the road separating the Carey compound from the horse corrals and barns. Across from the manager's home stood a two-story brick and stone building that served as the Carey family riding and carriage stables. South beyond the last horse barn, the road turned left down to the river, past the Careyhurst rail station by the ranch workers' family homes, the hayfields, and the cattle yards and barns. *This*, in his young, ambitious imagination, Clint said to himself, *will someday be mine to run.*

After breakfast, the cowboys gathered around Brown.

"We've got a tough ride today, up the north range in the canyon to round up about ten strays," said Brown. "Clint, go in the corral and bring us four of the best saddle horses."

Clint opened the corral gate and motioned to two corral men to join him with bridles. As he chose a horse, he bridled it and had one of the men take it to the gate. Soon he had four horses at the gate. He checked each horse's hooves to make sure they were well shod.

Brown took a quick look at all four and said, "Good, Clint. Frank, you're in charge. Take Clint, Big Bart, and Curly Jim. Saddle up, boys. Good ride. See you home this evening," said Brown.

They rode by the cookhouse, picked up lunches, and filled their canteens. In the chill of a late October morning, they rode up the hill above the Carey compound onto the high meadows.

It was almost six as they herded the ten strays into the cattle yard. Brown met them. "Good job, boys. Day's over. Your dinner is waiting up at the cookhouse."

Clint was dead tired, but he had made it all the way. He had proved his worth and never rode the range again. As he had showed his equine experience, he was given more and more responsibility for all the horses and mules. In December, he was made equine manager by Brown and Bob Carey, with a pay raise to fifty dollars a month.

It was time to get to a gunsmith and correct the wrong that had been done to him when he was robbed in the freight car. On a day off from work, he went to the Careyhurst rail station and got on the train bound for Douglas. There he found the gunsmith shop and spent some time carefully choosing his replacement .38, settling finally on a nice .38 Special with a soft-leather hip holster. Finally, he felt fully dressed.

Clint managed the needs of the ranch, having ready range saddle horses for the cowboys, work horse teams for the farm, spans of mules for the freight wagons, and the Carey family stable riding and carriage horses. He had a crew of four men, each expert in showing, grooming, and harness care.

But one of the cowboys under Clint's authority was proving to be a problem. The man went by the name "Frenchie," and while he did decent work when he was completely sober, it seemed that even a drop of whiskey turned him into a hothead with no judgment whatsoever.

One day Clint heard a commotion coming from the corrals. He had no trouble recognizing the sound of a mule in distress. Rushing to see what was amiss, he came upon Frenchie in a corral beating a mule with a two-by-four. Clint shouted, "Stop!" and jumped the wood railing. Enraged, he grabbed the two-by-four in one hand and Frenchie's shirt collar in the other. "We don't abuse animals here!" he yelled into the other man's face. "You're through! You're fired!" He walked Frenchie to the pay master to get his pay, and on the way out they ran into Curly Jim.

"Here, Curly Jim," said Clint. "Take this man off my hands before I tear his head off. See that he gathers up all his personal belongings, then take him out to the road and leave him there. He's through!"

Clint hoped never to see or hear of Frenchie again.

During the fall roundup and the spring herding of the yearling steers and heifers to the range land after branding, he provided the remuda, a rope corral of about twenty horses that moved with the cook and supply wagons. The remuda supplied remounts for the cowboys, giving them fresh rides for the long day moving the herd.

Clint placed one man full-time to manage the Carey stable. The tack room, carriages, and horses were always ready for the family and guests. Clint, though, paid special attention to Mrs. Carey. He would get her favorite horse saddled or, as she often requested, the one-horse shay hitched to the trotting horse. She took a liking to Clint and often asked him to saddle up and go with her down across the south meadow to the Platte River. There in the shade of the willow and cottonwood trees, they would dismount and sit on the soft grass near the water's edge. As they talked, she learned of Clint's interest in current events, reading newspapers, Europe, and South America. With a wink, she said, "Clint, it would have been so nice to have you with me in my travels." He knew she had already been around the world a couple of times, and she often brought gifts back for the children of Careyhurst.

Clint also learned about Mrs. Carey's youth and her marriage to Joseph Maull Carey. She had been born Louisa David in 1857 and was quite young when she married Joseph Carey. "He was twelve years older than I was, practically double my age when I met him," Mrs. Carey said with a laugh and a look of wonder on her face. She gave birth to the first of their two sons, Robert D. Carey, in 1878 when she was just twenty-one years of age. Her husband was from a wealthy manufacturing family in Delaware, and by the time she met him, he had already graduated from the University of Pennsylvania Law School and been appointed by President Ulysses Grant to the post of US Attorney for the Territory of Wyoming. After he moved west, he met and married Louisa and the two began a family.

From 1885 to 1890, Carey was a Territorial delegate to the US House of Representatives, where he sponsored a bill that resulted in statehood for Wyoming. Almost immediately, he was elected a US Senator from the new state, serving from 1890 to 1895. There, he sponsored the Carey Arid Lands Act, providing for cession of up to a million acres of arid federal lands to states that would irrigate them. His political and civic activities often kept him from home but were very important to Wyoming. "I understood that," Mrs. Carey told Clint. "And I knew it was my job to raise his sons and keep his home while he was away doing great work for our new state."

One of Carey's initiatives was the formation of the Wyoming Development Company, which built a long tunnel through the mountains to divert water from the Laramie River to irrigate the Wheatland Flats.

By 1910, Joseph Carey was Governor of Wyoming, supporting progressive reforms. As his term came to a close, their son Robert was showing signs of wanting to follow in his dad's political footsteps. Mrs. Carey's eyes sparkled as she told Clint stories about her husband and her sons.

It was autumn 1915 and an early October breeze moved through the high, bluestem grass meadow as Clint and Mrs. Carey rode back to the stables. As Clint helped her down from her saddle, she took his hand and said, "Thanks for a memorable afternoon. We must do this again soon."

While her grandchildren rarely visited the stables, her son Bob, manager of all the Carey ranch and farm properties, had an office on the second floor. He met with Clint about the need for horses and mules for the north ranch and farms, as well as where to find the best stallions and brood mares. They became fast friends, as Bob talked about his ambition to follow in his father's footsteps and someday become governor of Wyoming.

On a day off, Clint often joined with ranch hands and cowboys going to the gym and boxing arena in Glenrock. He was twenty-six and in the best physical condition of his life. Just five feet, nine and a half inches tall, he was broad-chested, with powerful forearms and rock-hard fists, foot size eight, great hand-eye coordination. At 160 pounds, he found he was a pretty fair middleweight boxer. His experience here would hold him in good stead in the future.

After their workout, most of them gathered down the block at Lola's Café and Piano Bar. His best friend, Frank, was not with them. He had been awarded his homestead land and had married the daughter of a Glenrock banker, who helped them prove up the land and build a small home and farm barns for his small herd of heifers and steers.

Once a month, Clint took his shay and best horse to Douglas for an overnight. After checking in at the hotel, he would go uptown to the barber shop for a shampoo, haircut, shave, manicure, and pedicure. Back at the hotel, he would join cowboy friends for dinner. But not always. Often he would walk up the hill to Rosie's place. Rosie's bordello was reputed to be the finest between Cheyenne and Casper. Her girls were not local. They were brought in from distant cities and rural towns by her husband, Ben, who was her procurer. Ben, a handsome man, skilled in his profession, dealt with other madams and was seldom home.

Rosie, an astute business woman, ran a very profitable house. She took sixty percent and provided full care of her girls, including monthly visits with Doctor Sanders. Dr. Sanders said the girls were all quite attractive, dressed in the latest fashions, but that their perfume, White Rose, was a bit much. When they left, he had to open the windows to air out the strong White Rose fragrance.

As Clint was leaving after his time with his favorite girl, Rosie stopped him. "Clint," she said, "won't you join me for a drink?"

"Of course, Rosie," Clint said, as she ushered him into her private office.

"Clint, I've heard good things about you and your work at Careyhurst," she said, as she poured two fingers of fine bourbon. "I need a good man like you to manage my properties. My husband is seldom home and is not a businessman. You will have an office downtown and I'll double your pay to start."

"I'm interested. Let me think about it, Rosie," said Clint.

"No hurry, Clint. Now be off with you down to the saloon and the game. Hold 'em and fold 'em. We will talk again soon," said Rosie.

Clint thought about Rosie's job offer: great pay, easy work, but he would be known as "Rosie's man." And he would always have the attention of the Sheriff. Not good, considering his Dodge City incident. The poker play went well. He went back to Careyhurst the next day with $200.

Over the holidays, he visited Frank and Meg. Their baby son, Frank Jr., was a year old. They lived in a comfortable ranch home. In the barns were saddle and work horses, and in the corral, fifty head of Herefords. He was in envy of them, but he still had his dream of a Nebraska grain, hay, cattle, and hog farm.

1917 dawned with the dark cloud of the war in France and Germany, and the threat of USA involvement steadily grew. President Wilson was arming the nation. With that effort came the draft, conscripting young men eighteen to thirty to build an invasion army. Clint, twenty-eight and single, knew he would be called soon.

Late May, he was in Douglas at the Saturday night poker game. Most of the talk was about being drafted. They had heard Teddy Roosevelt was coming out to enlist cowboys, reminiscent of his famed Rough Riders. There was, however, an effort to bring into one unit Converse County cowboys and ranch hands.

Just as they anted up for the next hand, in rushed Little Jim, Rosie's houseboy. "Mister Clinton, Rosie say you come up to the house. She needs your help now."

"What for?" said Clint.

"She don't say," said Jim.

"Well, boys, guess I better go. Check me out. I'll be back."

"Ben brought this woman in from Denver this afternoon. Something special for you, Clint."

Clint didn't reply, as he reached for his Stetson, jacket, and holstered .38. He left the saloon in a fast walk up to the house.

He was met at the door by Maude, Rosie's assistant, and ushered into Rosie's office. "Clint, I need your help," said Rosie. "Ben brought in a beautiful, young woman from Denver this afternoon. She has been making a terrible fuss from the moment she arrived. Says she is not *that* kind an entertainer. She keeps crying to me for her Clinton. 'He will help me!' Took me a while to realize 'her Clinton' might be you. Clint, I can't handle her. She is upstairs in Room 3. Would you go up and talk to her? Maybe you *are* her Clinton!"

Clint entered the room without knocking. A tearful, auburn-haired, young woman sat on the edge of the bed. She turned to Clint. Their eyes met and Clint said, "Marie, what are you doing here?"

Marie said, "Oh, Clint! I couldn't think of anyone but you. You have always come to my rescue."

"Marie, put your belongings together. I'll be right back to get you out of here."

Back down in Rosie's office, Clint said, "Rosie, I know her. She is a popular vaudeville pianist and singer. Haven't seen her in several years. I will take her off your hands and help her get home to her family in my hometown in Nebraska."

"Thanks so much, Clint. Next time you come, treats on me!"

Back up in the room, Marie was ready with her purse and small travel bag. Clint took her hand and said, "We are going down the outside backstairs. Watch your step."

At the bottom of the stairs, he turned and, holding her hand, walked in the dark around the house to the street. At the sidewalk, he took a railroad brakeman's lantern hanging from a hitching post. Using the lantern to guide them, they crossed the street and walked down the alleys three blocks to the stockyard and livery stable.

"Clint, where are you taking me?" Marie said.

"To my place, the Careyhurst Ranch," Clint said. "You will be safe there."

As they entered the stable, Clint said, "Marie, while the stable boy is getting my horse and shay, you best visit the ladies' room. We've a long ride ahead of us."

Clint had the stable boy wire a hook to the middle of the top of the shay. Clint hung the lantern there. It would help light the trail to Careyhurst.

He lifted Marie to the seat beside him and covered her with a wool blanket. "Marie, have you had anything to eat?"

"Not since early morning on the train," said Marie.

"We will stop at the stockyard café and I'll get ham sandwiches and coffee," said Clint.

Out on the trail, the horse took them on an easy slow-trot gait. As they ate, there was some small talk. "Marie, what brought you to Douglas?"

"Our vaudeville show broke up and I was left without a job. At the Brown Palace Hotel bar, I met this well-dressed businessman. I told him I was looking for work, that I had been the top act, performing my piano/vocal set. He said there was an opportunity for an attractive young woman in a bustling small city north of Cheyenne. 'I'm on my way to Douglas, leaving in the morning. Come with me. I think I can find work for you,' he said. So we left the next morning, bound to Douglas. I had no idea if it was hotel bar entertainment or in a theatre. I was broke and needed a job."

What Marie didn't tell Clint was that she had been living with Hans von Essen, brother of the man Clint shot when he rescued Marie out of Dodge City four years ago. Hans had a single acrobatic act and she was with him when the show folded. Hans wanted to return to Germany—it was his habit to go back to his homeland as often as he could. He had booked passage on one of the last passenger ships out of New York with protection

45

through the blockade to a German port. He gave her a hundred dollars, left her at the Brown Palace, and set out the next morning to New York en route to Germany.

Marie had thought it strange that Hans had little to say to her about the killing of his brother, Fredrik, when the two of them reunited some months after that fateful night in 1913. He had spoken very casually to her, asking just a few questions now and then about whether she had been alone, and, if not, who was with her. He seemed so calm, she saw nothing to prevent her from revealing, eventually, that it was Clint Morgan who had shot Fredrik but only in self-defense and to protect her. As far as she could tell, Hans accepted the news as if Clint's actions were reasonable and fitting. She hadn't learned until months later that Hans had collected his brother's body and accompanied the casket home to Germany, where he met with family and buried Fredrik. But Hans hadn't stayed long in his homeland. Increasing unrest there convinced him that he might be conscripted into the German army if he lingered. He soon returned to America, joining a vaudeville show that was working its way east to San Francisco and ultimately he found Marie again.

There was no hint in any of Hans's communications with Marie that he had taken a solemn vow to find and kill his brother's murderer.

Now Clint continued his effort to trace Marie's movements. "Did you stay with your sister in Oregon?" As he recalled that night, his last advice to her was to go to her sister.

"No," said Marie. "I went to Los Angeles, worked there and then to San Francisco. I had a great agent who got me engagements in theatre and hotel clubs."

Again, what she didn't tell Clint was about her affair with a high-class dancer and sometime stripper, Lily Lupino, who had, as described in her promotional posters, "a body to die for."

Lily worked in burlesque, gay clubs, and legitimate musical theatre. Marie and Lily were intimate lovers only briefly, but their affection for each other was intense and lasted for the rest of their lives.

"We are here," said Clint, as they came to the front atrium of the Carey Ranch mansion.

Despite the late hour, the house staff roused Mrs. Carey and she made her way down the stairs to the door.

"Mrs. Carey, I know it's very late … but this is Marie. Marie found herself in Douglas under some very unusual circumstances. She is from my hometown in Nebraska, and I wonder if you could have a place for her tonight. We'll talk tomorrow. If you could just have her for tonight, I'd really appreciate it."

Mrs. Carey said, "Of course, I'll help you, Clint. Come, my dear, let's go in." She took Marie downstairs to the housekeeper's rooms. There she introduced Marie to Leona, who took Marie to a vacant room for the night.

"Thank you, Mrs. Carey," said Clint. "We'll talk in the morning."

Clint left to put away the shay and unhitch his horse, get him fed and watered, then out into the open corral. Back in his apartment, Clint sat on the bed and suddenly realized that only one more day remained before he would be leaving with the Converse County Cowboys on their way to the AEF in France. *Oh, I must be with Marie. We'll only have tomorrow and tomorrow evening, and it's got to be a special evening.* He went to bed, slept very lightly, got up early, and made his plans for himself and Marie for the evening.

About ten in the morning, Clint walked over to the mansion and asked for Mrs. Carey. He and Mrs. Carey talked for a bit. Clint explained: "Marie was with her show in Denver when it broke up, and she thought she had an opportunity for her piano and vocal show in Douglas. Of course, it didn't turn out that way. She is a wonderful young lady."

Mrs. Carey interrupted, "Oh yes, we've already talked and she's going to be just fine."

Clint said, "Now, I need to talk to her, because I think we should be together this evening. It will be the only time that I have to be with her until I get back from France. As you know, the Cowboys are leaving tomorrow. Our time will be just tonight."

Mrs. Carey said, "Clint, I'll get Marie, and you two can talk for a bit."

Marie came upstairs. She had been downstairs unpacking some of her things.

Clint said, "Did you have a good evening and good night?"

She said, "Oh, I certainly did, Clint."

He said, "What I want you to do is get ready, wear your best, because we're going tonight to Glenrock to the Hotel Higgins. This will be our only time to be together because I have to leave tomorrow for France and the war. I'll be leaving with the Converse County Cowboys. It may be a long time before I get to see you again."

"Oh," Marie said. "Clint, I will be ready. Tell me what time."

Clint said, "I will have the shay ready. It's a short ride to Glenrock, so I'll be ready about six o'clock and pick you up here at the mansion."

Marie said, "I'll be ready, Clint. It will be so much fun!"

Early afternoon, Clint met with all of his co-workers. He explained to them that he would be gone and that he knew that they would all do well and take care of the remuda in his absence. "Either the ranch manager or Mr. Carey will be appointing one of you to be in charge in my absence."

He went back to his apartment fairly early to get cleaned up. He chose his best pair of Lucchese boots, his new blue boot-cut wool pants, white shirt, tie, his best Stetson, and jacket. Down at the corral, he made sure that his best horse was ready, then he got the shay ready—lantern and all. A few minutes before six, he was in front of the mansion, waiting for Marie.

Marie came out of the mansion with Mrs. Carey. Clint said, "Oh, Marie! You're so beautiful!"

Mrs. Carey said, "Well, Clint, make this a wonderful evening. You have a most delightful young woman to be with. Now, off with you!"

He helped Marie into the shay and they were on their way to Glenrock and the Hotel Higgins. It was a short ride, about forty-five minutes, and they didn't talk much. The anticipation was with them.

They got to the Higgins. Clint turned the horse and shay over to the houseboy. He registered for the best room upstairs with a private bath. Then he and Marie took their things up to the room. Marie looked around the room, with its bare floor, iron-post double bed, and single light bulb, and she thought to herself: *Well, it is not the Brown Palace—but I should care. I'm with Clint!*

They freshened up, then went down to the Antelope Bar. It was a little after seven. Marie said, "Oh my! Let's have a drink. And look! There's the piano. Let me play for you."

Clint said, "Oh, that would be terrific."

Marie sat down at the piano and began to sing and play a medley of popular songs, including "Good-Bye Broadway, Hello France," "Over There," "That's the Kind of a Baby for Me," "Yaddie Kaddie Kiddie Kaddie Koo," and "It's a Long, Long Way to Tipperary." Clint and all the rest of the folks joined around the piano, singing along, and applauded with tremendous enthusiasm.

It was quite a crowd in the bar, enjoying Marie's playing. Several were businessmen and their wives who were hotel guests, and intermingled among them were engineers and others associated with the oil industry. Since oil had been found in a successful discovery well the previous year on public lands near Glenrock, an oilfield known as the "Big Muddy" had gone into production. Mutual Oil Company was building a refinery, so more new faces were showing up every day. It was fair to say that an oil boom had resulted, and the establishments that served strangers and guests to the town of Glenrock were also booming.

Off to one side in the bar that evening were a couple of second-generation British ranchers, older men who had survived the devastating blizzard of 1887. They were enjoying Marie's singing and playing as much as the rest, but the toll of what they had endured was visible on their faces.

Clint had grown up hearing about the blizzard that changed forever the vast expanses of open range grazing land. Scores of hopeful would-be ranchers had come years before to Wyoming and the regions around it, including the sons of a few wealthy British families who hoped to stake a claim in the American West. With their wealth, they brought in huge herds of cattle, branded them, and let them roam the open range for grass. These families were in their second generation as ranchers when the summer of 1886 came, so hot that the sun scorched the prairies. The herds were already hungry from inadequate grazing when the snows began falling that winter. The blizzard that came in January 1887 covered the range in nearly a foot and a half of snow. Temperatures dropped too. Very few of the ranchers had hay for feed and certainly not enough for the herds they had accumulated.

Millions of cattle died either from the weather or from starvation. Only the cattle that managed to reach the relative safety of the Nebraska Bad Lands found enough shelter to survive. Bankruptcy forced most of the British who had come to the plains to return where they had come from, but a fortunate few salvaged enough of their herds to survive and stay. Of these were the British voices that joined in the singing that night in the Antelope Bar at the Hotel Higgins.

Finally Clint signaled to Marie that the performance must end if they were to make their dinner reservations, which he had made in the Paisley Shawl for eight o'clock. The crowd applauded and cheered for her, with whistles of appreciation mixed in, when she gave a small, elegant salute to close the show.

Clint and Marie went across the hall to the restaurant of the fine hotel. There in the dining room was their table with white linen setting off the dark-wood chairs. As they were seated, Marie looked around in surprise, thinking: *Why, this is better than the Brown Palace!* Bubbling champagne was freshly poured into flutes—everything was ready for them. They toasted with the champagne and listened to the small orchestra playing. He knew she was keeping an eye on the dance floor. As an unexpected adventure, Clint danced with Marie, something both knew he wasn't normally inclined to do.

Their dinner was the five-course continental cuisine, by special service. Marie gazed around the elegant room, taking in the two large windows on the back wall, and another two to their left. Antelope antlers stood tall in one corner, while in the opposite stood an Oriental screen. A table at the back wall stood in front of a large painting of a woman in a shawl. Clint could see her trying to memorize the details of this special night.

When later a young woman with a camera came to their table, they arranged a place for the two of them to have their picture taken together, as a lasting memory.

About ten, they went up to their room, retired, and began to speak quietly of their plans. Clint promised to come back to her at the earliest opportunity. Marie promised that she would be there for Clint when he came home from France. She said that Mrs. Carey would have a job for her and help her get entertainment jobs in Cheyenne. In return, she would help Mrs. Carey at the mansion, providing piano lessons for the children and entertaining at Mrs. Carey's social events.

Clint said, "Well, it's been a long time, the two of us together. When I come home, I know I'll have the opportunity to be the general manager of Careyhurst. I still, perhaps, will qualify for the Homestead Land Grant, like Frank, my friend, has done. We'll have a great future together, Marie."

Marie said, "Oh, Clint. This is so wonderful! I don't want to travel anymore. I want to be with you. I've always wanted to be with you."

Clint said nothing but took her in his arms and their lovemaking was all that they could ever have dreamed of as they went on through the night.

In the morning, in order to keep on time, Clint had to get up early and get on the way, because that afternoon he was leaving for France. A little after seven, he went downstairs and asked the houseboy to get the shay. He took care of the bill. As Marie dressed, she thought about her home in San Francisco. Though she was so in love with Clint, she missed Lily and their good times in the city. She thought about that and wondered if she would ever be able to see Lily again.

Then Clint and Marie went down to the dining room but ordered just coffee and toast. Marie, glowing, said, "Clint, let's go home." And so they returned to Careyhurst.

He left Marie at the mansion and went back to his place to pack and get everything together that he needed to have saved for him. Upstairs in the main stables, he found a compartment with a lock and there he stored the lantern, his special riding boots, and the clothes he would need when he returned.

That afternoon, the cowboys gathered down at the Careyhurst Station. Frank McDuffie was there to see them off. When Clint and Marie came in from the ranch, Clint introduced Marie to Frank, who said, "Oh, this is the beautiful woman you've told me so much about. Yes, Clint, we'll make sure everything is taken care of and, Marie, we'll see that you're well cared for. We want you to come out and visit us at our place."

Marie said, "I would love to."

Then they had all gathered at the station—the folks from the ranch, Bob Carey, Mrs. Carey, the ranch manager, and all their friends—to wish them well.

Cowboys Big Bart and Curly Jim were also part of the Converse County contingent and joining Clint. They were off to the side with their friends, with their good-byes and enjoying a little libation.

In such a place ... it is still possible to hear
the sad sweet music of time
— Simon Schama

CHAPTER 4
WORLD WAR I INTERRUPTS THE COURSE OF LIFE

The train whistle blew, signaling that it was time to move. Hand-in-hand with Marie and Mrs. Carey, Clint got ready to board. He and Marie shared a good-bye hug and kiss, and Mrs. Carey gave him a hug. She said, "Clint, we're going to miss you. We'll take care of Marie. Clint, I love you. Come home." Then Clint turned to board the train. Marie walked away, hand-in-hand with Mrs. Carey, both of them in tears.

Clint, Big Bart, and Curly Jim arrived at the Douglas Depot and joined the cowboys on a trip that would take them east to the port and on their way to France. On their way east, they picked up more draftees and enlistees, and when they arrived at the port in Newport News, some of the new troops went for special basic training. The cowboys had initial processing, underwent their physicals, received all their equipment, and suffered through a day or two of orientation. They boarded the troop train for a very short ride to the port where the converted passenger liner was now their troop ship. They started out on their voyage to France.

Their first day out, they were assigned to lifeboat checks and more orientation. Most of the cowboys and many of the troops had never seen a body of water like the Atlantic Ocean. The most they had ever seen, perhaps, was a pond where the cattle watered up in the hills, or the Platte River. So it was a very new experience for all.

During the lifeboat drill, Clint was lined up on the deck with the others, fastening their life jackets. Next to Clint was a very young cowhand, eighteen (probably really seventeen) years old, and he was having a lot of problems trying to get his life jacket fastened right. A grizzled old deckhand came up to him, studied the problems he was having, and said, "Son, you got a lot of time. Don't worry about it. The ship won't sink for about another five minutes." With that, the young boy turned chalk white and hit the deck in a faint. The deckhands thought it was really funny. But one old deckhand helped him up, got a little bit of water on his face, got him a cup of water, fixed his life jacket, and said to Clint: "Take this man down to the galley deck to get something to eat. Fix him up; he's going to be okay."

Now, the trip was a nice, easy run as Atlantic crossings go. Not much happened; a little bit of seasickness by some of the boys—but they did okay and soon the coast of France came into view. There was their port where they came in to debark. This was the Port of Brest, France. They unloaded and were put on a French *quarante et huit* (40&8) troop train, one composed of the four-wheel, covered goods wagons, each designed to hold forty men or eight horses. From there, they were taken to Abbeville, where they joined the Fifth Veterinary Corps Hospital, supporting the 10th Cavalry.

They settled in at the hospital. The next day Clint was assigned to work with one of the veterinarians. Having watched

Clint for a while, the veterinarian said, "Young man, you seem to know a lot about the horses."

Clint said, "Yes. I've had a little experience, working with my father, who is a horse and mule trader, and I know one of the best old veterinarians, Doc Graves."

The veterinarian said, "Oh, Doc Graves, a great equine doctor! He was the best but had a little bit of a problem, a little bit of a heavy drinker, but he was really good."

In addition, Clint was assigned to the Veterinary Medical Supply as a clerk. There he worked nearly every day.

About three weeks after they arrived was the first mail call. Letters from home! Clint's name was called out for a letter from Marie. He opened the letter, which had been written the day that they'd left Douglas. She wrote:

> *We're doing very well, Clint, and I hope you're okay. I'll miss you and we all want you to be home soon. I am doing well with my work with Mrs. Carey and waiting for you so that when you come home, we will be together again.*
>
> *With all my Love,*
> *Marie*

Clint's heart swelled so much, reading and rereading that letter, it felt like it might just burst in his chest. He touched with soiled fingers where she had signed her name. Yes, that's what he wanted: all Marie's love. That was all he wanted.

On his first day off, Clint went into Abbeville. As he walked through, seeing the shops, a gift and jewelry shop attracted his eye. He walked in and saw something that really interested him. It was a presentation of a 20-franc gold coin, with a story beside it. As he was looking at it, the owner of the shop came over and said, "Here, let me help you. I'll translate that story. It is called The Lucky Gold Angel."

Clint listened as the shop owner read. The legend of the coin involved a condemned man who was saved from the guillotine during the French Revolution and who attributed his good fortune to the 20-franc gold coin in his pocket. The coin was for remembrance and good luck.

Clint purchased the coin and its presentation package. The clerk furnished a special envelope for it. Then he wrote a message to Marie:

I didn't have a chance to get anything for you before I left. Let this be a remembrance for both of us, as we think about each other until the time we are able to be together again. I love you very, very much.

Love, Clint

As the time went on, there were other mail calls, but no more letters from Marie. He did not understand; he couldn't figure out what was going on. He had written to his friend Frank but had no answer from him either. Clint never received another letter from Marie. He just couldn't believe it. He wondered: *Could it have been just like Marie to do the same thing she did before, when she suddenly changed and left and I didn't know what was going to happen?*

To help get his mind off his disappointment and worry, he focused on a competition coming up between the various veterinarian hospitals. Clint got involved and found out that his experience in boxing back home served him well. He became his unit's middleweight champion and was preparing to go to the big competition for a chance to be the division middleweight champion.

On a lazy afternoon in early October, Clint was going through the inventory of the medical supplies in the pharmacy. Supplies were being used up rapidly because of the heavy fighting at the front. As he turned and looked up, there standing in front of him was a tall, dark-haired captain of the medical corps. Clint recognized him immediately: "Wes!"

Wes looked at Clint: "Well, Clint! Where have you been?"

It was Wesley Lowe, Carrie's eldest brother and Clint's friend from home whom he hadn't seen in more than ten years.

"Wes, tell me: what have you been doing and what is going on at home?"

Wes said, "Well, Clint, Carrie is single again. I was married too, but, unfortunately, I just lost my wife, Edith, in the Great Flu Epidemic. It's been very difficult. We've also had some very tough times at the front lines. I hope this thing is over soon."

Clint expressed condolences and agreed about the war, then he said, "But tell me about Carrie."

Wes said, "Carrie was widowed about two years ago. The man she married had taken her to a little community near Sioux City. While he traveled with his racing dogs and worked at the main tracks with horses, Carrie was living mostly alone with two little babies, a daughter not yet two years old and a son not yet a year old. One night her husband, as he was coming home— apparently having had too much to drink—went off the road and crashed, and the steering wheel of his Model T crushed his chest. He died at the hospital in Sioux City. Fortunately, he had a little bit of life insurance, enough for Carrie to go back to Pender and buy a little home. She's been doing the only thing she knew to make a living, and that's cooking and preparing meals, which she learned when she worked for the Nye family. She started a little boarding house, offering meals for the teachers and businessmen of the community. Clint, she misses you and I know she often wonders about you. You really should get in touch with her."

Clint said, "Well, Wes, I've made another commitment. Do you remember Marie?"

"Oh, I sure do."

"Well, she and I have been in touch with each other for a long time and now she's at the ranch in Wyoming at Careyhurst and waiting for me to get home. We hope to be married."

Wes said, "Well, that's really wonderful. In the meantime, how are things going here for you, Clint?"

Clint said proudly, "I have gotten involved with boxing and I am the middleweight champion of our unit. We're going to have the final division championships here next month, about the middle of November. If you can get some time free—I'm not sure exactly where it's going to be, but you can help me and wish me luck."

Wes said, "Well, sure. Let's see what we can do. I'll be back to see you soon."

It turned out that Clint saw Wes sooner than either of them had expected.

Clint was spending every free minute training, which meant taking on every preliminary boxing match he could get himself into. In one of those matches leading up to the middleweight championship, he encountered an unexpected opponent, a cowboy who already had a grudge against Clint from a nasty encounter at Careyhurst years earlier.

Clint went to the match neither knowing nor caring who his opponent would be. His mind's eye was so focused on the eventual championship match that he barely saw who he was boxing in the intermediate matches.

Déjà vu swept over him when he stepped into the ring. He shook his head to clear the sensation, but then he realized: *No, it's not déjà vu; I really have seen this character before. And he wasn't good news then either.* It was Frenchie, the cowboy Clint had fired on the spot for beating a mule with a two-by-four.

Immediately all of Clint's senses were on high alert. He could see by the look in Frenchie's eyes that his opponent had taken this match on purpose to have a chance to even the score.

Frenchie glared pure hatred at Clint, and when his boxing gloves came up to protect his face, the hatred still shone unmistakably. When the bell ended Round 1, Frenchie taunted in a high-pitched voice that only Clint could hear: "Oh, Marie, Marie. You're my woman, Marie." Clint struggled to focus on boxing and not lash out in blind fury.

The taunts grew uglier as Frenchie left his corner for Round 2. Now rather than mimicking Clint talking to Marie, he spoke in his own deep, gravelly voice: "That little woman you left at Careyhurst has been having a great time with the boys. *All* the boys." He took advantage of Clint's shock to land a good punch to the side of Clint's head. Now Clint's gloves were back where they needed to be, and he landed a solid right into his opponent's mouth. When the bell signaled the end of the round, Frenchie snarled into his ear: "She won't be worth much by the time you get back." Then he spat blood, hitting Clint's boxing shoe, before going to his corner.

But Frenchie—whose judgment had always been lousy—had crossed a line. When the bell rang for the third round, Clint sprang out of his own corner and slammed into Frenchie with the force of a freight train. A blindingly hard right to the jaw was followed by a stunning left jab to the middle of Frenchie's face that brought a satisfying crunch of nose cartilage and a spurt of red in every direction. Even though Frenchie's left eye was already beginning to close, Clint could see his eyes cross and roll upward as he went down to the mat. The referee stopped the match. Clint had won. His only regret was that Frenchie was still alive.

But Frenchie wasn't done. One night two weeks later when Clint was on duty at the veterinary pharmacy, Frenchie stumbled in, drunk and angry, and came at Clint with a bayonet. Clint took no time to think about it; he pulled his .45 from his shoulder holster and shot Frenchie, killing him instantly.

The shot brought the guards running. Clint was relieved of his .45 and escorted to the guardhouse. A court-martial hearing was scheduled, giving Clint only a couple of days to locate Wes and get him on board for legal representation. In the course of the investigation, it came to light that Frenchie had been making a regular practice of stealing medical supplies from the pharmacy and selling them on the French black market.

The court decided that Clint had acted in self-defense. Wes said, "I think everyone here is mostly interested in making sure you're not in the guardhouse but in the boxing ring for the championship."

Though Clint was free to go, his sergeant stripes were taken away and his rank was reduced to private. "What?! Why did they do that?" Clint asked. Wes told him that this was an outcome he should have expected. It was a matter of military discipline, Wes said, because he had shot first rather than calling the guards for assistance. "Well, of course I shot first. I would be dead now if I hadn't!"

Wes warned him: "Now keep your mouth shut and don't fight about it. You're not going to win this one."

"Looks like I didn't win the other one either," Clint said.

Losing his stripes was much worse than any blow Clint had taken in the ring. Now he needed all the more to win the middleweight championship to restore his pride. He doubled up on training and preparation, spending every moment he could getting ready for the big match.

Then November 11 came—the Armistice—and all things changed. Amid the cheering and the flowing wine, it suddenly dawned on Clint: there would be no boxing match, no competition between the veterinarian hospitals. Everybody's thoughts were on closing down and going home. In his entire time in France, Clint had never gone near the front lines, and now his one shot at the boxing championship was also taken away.

Later in November, Wes came by. They talked for a bit and Clint said, "Wes, what are you going to do now?"

He said, "Well, I don't know. I'm just not thinking about anything except staying here in France. I'm not going to go back—at least not right away. I think I'm going to go to Paris. I think I'll stay there and see what I can do that will get me away from everything. Maybe I'll try to get with a band. As you know, we Lowe boys are not so good but that we can't do well as musicians, and I would hope that I could use my ability with my guitar and particularly my singing voice."

Clint nodded. "Maybe that's what you ought to do."

After a moment of silence, Wes said, "What about you?"

"I don't know what I'm going to do, except that I hope that I get back and possibly when I do get home, I can try my hand at professional boxing. Beyond that, I want to get back to the ranch. I have to get myself reestablished." Neither felt like joining in the loud jubilation around them. "Let's be sure to keep in touch," Clint said, and that was how they parted.

Wes did go to Paris, and he lived in Paris until 1921, coming home to their hometown in the fall of 1921.

Clint, with the Converse County Cowboys, left France in 1919 around the first of June, and arrived by troop ship going home to their port in Newport News. Clint had a couple of days in Newport News before all the troops went to various separation centers. He took his time and went on up into New Jersey to a professional boxing club to see what he might do. It took fewer than a half-dozen bouts for him to learn that his age— he was now thirty—was against him and boxing was not going to be the way to his future.

Back in Newport News, he joined the rest of the cowboys and took the train back to Douglas. He went with the other boys to Fort Russell in July 1919 and got his honorable discharge and his final pay of $104. At the gate of the fort, Clint was met by Jack Nelms, who was the driver for Bob Carey, now Governor Carey, and his Twin-Six Packard. Jack drove him to Careyhurst.

Bob Carey welcomed him home, not wasting much time on preliminaries. He said, "Clint, you have a job waiting here for you. Brown's retired and Jim Smith has been managing here in the interim. My son, Bob Jr., is helping also. Now, the job of general manager of Careyhurst is yours, if you want it."

After a moment, Clint said, "Well, I believe I'll take the job, Governor. Let's get started."

Governor Carey said, "Come on up to the office. We'll go through some things. We'll get you settled, and then I have to get back to Cheyenne."

After the meeting with Bob Carey, Clint found his things that he had stored in 1917 and gathered everything up. His apartment was still there, and he moved in. The first thing he wanted to find out, though, was what happened to Marie. Mrs. Carey was not there; she was home in Cheyenne. Clint thought: *Well, let me see what Frank has to say.*

The next day he found the old shay and his horse and went up to Frank's ranch. There Frank greeted him and introduced his new little family. Frank and his wife were so happy to see Clint. They both wanted to learn about his experience in France, but Clint wanted to find out what happened to Marie. "I can't seem to find out anything about her," he told Frank.

Frank said, "We don't know. All we know is that she had been working with Mrs. Carey and in late 1918, in September maybe it was, she got up one morning, packed and got on one of the freight wagons that were on their way to Douglas and we've not heard from her since. We just don't know."

Clint said, "Well, I guess that's Marie. I just don't understand it." Then he said, "Now, how are things at the ranch?"

Frank said, "Oh, we're doing very well. My son here now will soon be four, and, look, our little daughter is just a little over one year old. We're so happy."

Clint said, "Oh, yes. That's terrific news." He looked at Frank with his family. He didn't doubt that Frank was happy, but there was something he couldn't put his finger on. Something was just slightly off center, not quite right. He decided there must be some issue about the ranch that Frank wasn't willing to share with him. Of course, that was Frank's right, to keep his own counsel.

"And what are you doing now?" Frank asked him.

"I just got through meeting with Governor Carey, and he named me the new general manager of Careyhurst, so it looks like I'll be around and probably be seeing more of you."

Frank said, "Oh, that's just wonderful. And I wish you all of the best, Clint." Frank's right hand rested on his son's shoulder, and his left, on the little girl's head.

Back at Careyhurst the next day, Clint met with Jim Smith and they went over the things that had been going on the past six months. Jim went through everything with him, then said, "Bob's son spends most of his time in Cheyenne, but he does come up once in a while, and I think we're doing very well. If you need some help, I'll be glad to help you in any manner you need."

Clint said, "Well, let's get with it."

So they toured all the ranch: the horse corrals on down to the fields and cattle yards, and met with part of the staff. As he talked with Jim, Clint could tell that Jim was not particularly happy. He knew that Jim thought that he might be the one who would be appointed manager. *I'm sure it's a disappointment to him.*

As time went on, this was going to become a more difficult problem, and Clint soon sensed that things were not going to be as easy as he'd thought they might be.

Time moved on through the rest of 1919 and into 1920. Clint would meet with Governor Carey to go over what needed to take place in annual roundups and the sale of livestock and some of the new ventures with the farm. Among these was the raising of hogs and the culture of the swine, which was now a new cash crop for Careyhurst.

Then on a Monday morning in the middle of June 1922, Bob called from the governor's office to talk to Clint. He said, "The family and I are coming up this coming Sunday to visit. My mother and father, and my wife, and my daughter Deborah, and I think my son will be there too. Try to have things in good order. I'd like to meet with you about business and the like, then we can tour the ranch."

Clint said, "Everything will be taken care of, Bob. I'll have everything ready."

About ten Sunday morning, the family arrived, all in Bob's new Packard, driven by Nelms, his chauffeur. They stopped at the mansion. Bob met with Clint and they spent some time up in the office. And then Bob said, "I'd like to talk to some of the boys."

Clint said, "Good. Now, most of them are out at the spring range. But the senior cowboys, whom you know, are all over there at the corral."

So, Bob and Clint went over to the corral and Bob stopped and talked with each one a little bit. They had all been with the ranch ten years or more.

Later Bob returned to the mansion to rejoin the family, and Clint went over to the main corral. He got the carriage ready and the four-horse hitch. Then he went over to the mansion. Bob and Mrs. Carey and Mr. Carey Sr. all got into the carriage. Clint took the reins and Bob rode up on the buckboard with him.

They toured the ranch, around the mansion and the main corral barns, down to the farm, around through the farm and the corrals, then across and back up into the hills way above the Platte River to the high country and across, and then back down and along the Platte and back up to the mansion and the ranch. They all got out and Mrs. Carey said, "Now, Clint, you're coming in with us. We're going to have a picnic dinner. It's been a long time since I've seen you, Clint. We've got to catch up on things."

So Clint gave the reins to one of the boys, who took over the care of the horses and putting the carriage away. Clint followed the Careys, and there on the lawn out from the house by the running stream was a beautiful picnic dinner. Mrs. Carey sat next to Clint. She said, "Tell me, Clint, how are things going?"

Clint said, "Well, doing very well except I sure miss Marie and I don't know what happened to her."

Mrs. Carey said, "No, we don't know. We miss her. But I miss *you* so much. I just got back from a cruise to South America, Clint, and I had a wonderful time. It would have been nice if you could have been with me. I went to Colombia. I even brought some birds back with me for my aviary at the house in Cheyenne. Now, I don't come up here much anymore, you know. Mr. Carey is getting along in years, and we kind of have to take care of each other, so I won't be seeing you as much as I once did. I want you to take care of yourself and do well, and I know you will."

Through the dinner, he spoke a bit with Mr. Carey Sr. and then with Bob. The family left about four in the afternoon for the trip back to Douglas and Cheyenne. Clint was so pleased that they had come. It had been a wonderful break in the routine and made him feel like he was appreciated in his work at the ranch. In fact, he started to feel that things weren't quite so bad after all.

It was seldom that Bob Carey's son showed up at the ranch. He came once in a while but showed very little interest in what needed to be done or in any responsibilities of managing. Jim Smith seemed to prefer a friendship with Carey Jr., and the two of them typically separated off by themselves. Clint, because of everything else he had to take care of, at first did not pay much attention to this development. He thought that things were doing well; he wanted to keep busy, especially since he was alone, without Marie, and was trying to make the best of things with all the responsibility he had for the entire operation of Careyhurst.

It was a Monday morning in March 1923. Clint, after a weekend in Douglas, was up early, anxious to get underway with the week's work. He and Jim Smith rode down to the farm and cattle yards. As he looked over to the first corral, Clint said to Jim, "Where are the Herefords? That corral had fifteen prize polled Hereford heifers ready to go with the herd out to the spring range."

"We sold them Saturday," Smith said.

"You what?!" Clint said. "On whose orders?"

"Bob Carey Jr. was here, and these buyers came in with him. At the time, I thought the Governor had ordered the sale. It was odd, though, because they went for ten percent under market price."

Stunned, Clint asked, "Neither one of you tried to call me?"

"No," said Jim.

Clint had never fully trusted Jim Smith, and he did not really know Carey Jr. It made no difference now. He knew Bob would be furious. He rode back to his office. A call from Bob was waiting for him.

"Clint, what happened? Why did you sell those Herefords? We lost three thousand dollars on that sale!"

Clint interrupted. "Bob, I wasn't here, and I don't yet know the truth of what happened."

"This is unforgivable. You're the manager. You're supposed to be in charge."

Clint swallowed and looked off through the window toward the horizon. He knew what he had to do, but it was leaving a bad taste in his mouth.

"Bob, please accept my resignation and authorize my final check. I shall be gone by tomorrow morning. I am going home to Nebraska. Thank you for all you have done for me these last ten years. I have given you my best, always." He put the phone down quietly, ending the connection before Governor Carey could speak further.

Clint took the next couple of hours to put his files and desk in order, then he left his keys on the desk. He walked over to his house and found his housekeeper waiting at the door.

"Marge," Clint said, "I am leaving early in the morning. If you would help me get packed, I'd appreciate it." He went over to the pay master's office, where his check was ready: $450 for March and half of April.

Jim Smith went into the office after Clint left, sure that he would be the new manager. He was fired that afternoon.

Early Tuesday morning, Curly Jim had the shay ready. Clint loaded his two bags and the lantern. Curly took him to the station in Douglas. They shook hands, and Clint asked him to thank all the cowboys on his behalf. Then he bought a ticket on the morning train, east to Sioux City.

Once on the train, riding through the ranch country of western Nebraska, Clint thought about his life in the past ten years and wondered how things would be for him in Nebraska. He remembered when he had left his father, Chauncy, and the horse and mule train on that fateful evening in Dodge City. He relived the escape with Marie, getting her away safely. His memories took him on through the summer, to Careyhurst and his good fortune of getting his job at Careyhurst that carried him through all those years, through World War I, when he had believed he would go home to be with Marie. But Marie not only did not wait for him; she had completely disappeared.

Now, as his hometown grew closer, he found himself thinking: *What happened to Carrie? When I get home to Pender, what will I find?*

At the depot in Pender, Nebraska, he saw a familiar face. It was Artie, the young man who had delivered his telegram ten years earlier. Artie was at the desk. He was now the depot agent and he was busy at the telegraph. He waved at Clint; Clint waved back.

Clint walked all through the deport with his luggage: two bags and his lantern. Outside, up from the lumberyard and the granaries, he saw the old Lindell Hotel. He opened the door and walked into the lobby, and there was Mrs. Smith at the desk. It was as though the hotel had been frozen in time for ten years. She looked up and said, "Well, Clint! You've been gone a while. You're back."

"Yes," said Clint. "I am. Do you still have my luggage and everything?"

"Well, we sure do. And I think maybe I might have your room. Tell me: all this time, where have you been?"

"Oh, I've been back in Wyoming—a lot of different places."

"Well, we'll talk about that later," said Mrs. Smith. "Let's get your luggage, get everything together here, get you your room, so that you can get yourself fixed up a little bit. I think you're probably tired. You must have had that long train ride. Where did you come from?"

"Douglas," Clint said. "Douglas, Wyoming."

"Oh my. Well, you can take care of yourself here and we'll talk about how we can do this. If you're going to be here for a while, we'll get you fixed up with a good monthly rate, Clint."

"Okay. Thank you so much, Mrs. Smith."

Clint sat on the bed for a few minutes, then opened his luggage and started to put his things where they belonged. Then he got cleaned up a little bit. By then he was curious how the town might have changed. *Well, I think I'll just go uptown and look around.* As he left the hotel and went back up the street, up past the barbershop, to the saloon—of course, it was closed (Prohibition, you know)—past the bank, past a couple of offices, the stores, Johnny Meyer's special butcher shop, Mr. Predmetsky's general store. As he walked on down, he thought: *I'm going to try to find Carrie. I think I know where her house is.*

Wes had pretty well described where it might be, and Clint remembered that area near the high school. He kept walking several blocks, feeling his anticipation grow. Then he saw the little house there on the corner. *That must be Carrie's place.*

He walked across the street, up to the front door, and knocked on the door. Carrie came to open the door. She said, "Oh, it's Clint. Oh, Clint. How nice to see you!"

"Yes, Carrie. It's me."

We love the things we love for what they are
— Robert Frost

CHAPTER 5
GATHERING THE THREADS OF A NEW LIFE

It seemed at first that she could only stare at him. "Well, Clint
… well … where have you been? I've missed you so much.
Come on in. Come in, Clint. Oh my! Oh my!"

And Clint then took her into his arms and said, "It's been
so long, Carrie. Let's see what we can do to remember each
other."

"Yes, Clint." There they spent an hour. Then Carrie said,
"I must be getting dinner ready for all my guests. Now, you just
stay here. Wes's going to be here this evening, and we're going
to have a great evening."

As Carrie started the dinner, her two children came into
the house from outside, where they had been playing with
friends after school. Clarabelle was nine years old, and Ardell,
seven. She took them into the living room and said, "Children, I
want you to meet a very dear friend of mine, Mr. Clint Morgan."

Now, Clint was a bit uncomfortable because he hadn't
been near youngsters for a very long time, but it was just a few
minutes before they sat with him on the lounge and started
asking a lot of questions and he was telling them some western

stories of Wyoming and his cowboy days. He noted that Ardell had a great deal of difficulty walking, and Carrie explained, "He's just getting over polio, Clint. He's had a very difficult time, but we're going to make it."

As the evening came on, she had the table set for ten, and the dinner was almost ready. The boarders and guests started coming in, and there came in Wes—Wes and his new wife, Irene. Wes said, "Oh, here's Clint! You did come home, Clint. Well, I want you to meet my new wife, Irene. She is the English teacher at the high school, and we've been married just a short time. As you know, I came back from Paris a little over a year ago. I'm working. I've been doing construction work and I'm thinking of running for sheriff. Here in the dining room with my sister, I met this wonderful woman, Irene, and she is going to be my wife now forever and ever."

At the dinner, there were many other guests, many of whom Clint did not remember or recognize. Young businessmen, some of the folks from the courthouse, the county judge and his wife, among other folks. It was a delightful evening, and as the dinner ended and the guests left the house, Clint, Wes, and Irene helped Carrie with the dishes and getting things cleaned up in the kitchen. Then Ardell and Clarabelle were sent to their rooms to finish homework, and the four adults had a chance to talk and get acquainted again, talking about old times and the things that they planned.

As the evening went on, Carrie was obviously quite tired, and so was Clint. Clint said, "You know, I have to have some rest. I am going to excuse myself. I'm staying at the Lindell Hotel. You would know that that's where I would be. And I'm going to be able to see you tomorrow, Carrie. Will that be all right?"

"Oh, Clint! I can hardly wait."

It was near ten o'clock in the evening, and Wes and Irene had left a few minutes earlier. Clint said to Carrie, "It's been a long day and so wonderful, but I must get back to the hotel and get things situated. Now, I'm going to see you tomorrow."

Carrie said, "You come back for dinner, if not earlier."

As Clint left the house and walked across the street, Carrie stood at the door and thought: *How wonderful! I know he still loves me, and that we are going to be together now forever.*

The next morning, Clint was up early and had a cup of coffee at the hotel. He went on up to the restaurant on Main Street and had breakfast. Sure enough, in came his old friend, Duncan Laird. He saw Clint and came over and said, "Oh, my boy! You're home! Why have you taken such a long time to come home? What have you been doing?" He took the chair opposite Clint and signaled to have a cup of coffee brought to him.

Clint said, "Well, been out in Wyoming in ranch country, and now I'm back."

Duncan listened as Clint talked about his experiences. "You'll have to come out to the farm, Clint. We can have a Scotch there and make a proper toast to your return." He lifted his coffee cup, nodded toward his young friend, and quoted his favorite poet:

> *And now I have lived—I know not how long!*
> *And still I can join in a cup or a song;*
> *But whilst with both hands I can hold the glass steady,*
> *Here's to thee, my hero, my sodger laddie!*

They raised their coffee cups to that, then Duncan asked: "Do you still have that lifelong dream of that land up north and east? You know, it's still there. It hasn't opened up yet. Now, what are you going to be doing, Clint?"

So Clint talked about the new methods of farming he had learned from the Careyhurst agricultural research on the farmlands along the Platte River. He knew he could make good use of that knowledge. Then he said, "I want to see Carrie more. I saw her last night, and I think I'm going to plan things."

Duncan nodded his approval. "You know, I have seen Carrie at church many times, and she is very well thought of in our church—you know, the Presbyterian."

"Yes, I know."

Then Duncan asked him, "Well, do you want to come out and work with me for a little bit? Whatever you'd like to do. I know we'll be seeing each other." As they stood to part, Duncan said, "Give it some thought and let me know. Can't get to the saloon anymore, but maybe sometime we'll have a nice Scotch that we can share. We'll just hear some poetry and review old times. See ya soon."

Clint walked through the town and thought about what he ought to be doing. He was a little uncomfortable. In his pockets were his savings, all that cash, a little over $2,000. He was not comfortable with having any of it put into a bank but he really didn't want to be carrying it around with him. So, he stopped in at Pender State Bank. He scowled as he crossed the lobby. He didn't like the president of the bank, but he had a good friend who worked there, one of the vice presidents, Paul McAdams, and Paul greeted him: "Gee, Clint! Tell me about yourself. We haven't seen you in so long." He and Clint talked.

Clint said, "Yes, you know, I'm a little wary of this, but I have a little bit of cash. Do you suppose I could kind of set up an account? Maybe earn a little bit of interest until I decide what I'm going to do?"

"We can take care of you, Clint, and you can be sure it's going to be safe."

So, Clint made a deposit, opening an account for right at $2,000.

McAdams said, "Well, that's pretty good, Clint. You've done quite well for yourself."

Clint said, "I've saved a little money, and I've got a lot of good experience. I think I'm going to try to get up north and, hopefully someday soon, try to find the Indian land that I've always wanted. I'm going to see what we can do. I'm going to see Carrie again this evening for dinner. You all might want to come as a guest with me."

Later in the morning, Clint walked on down to the livery stable. What he had in mind was getting a good horse and saddle. It was a crisp March day with a little snow on the ground but not so bad. He thought: *You know, I think I'll just ride on up north and see what I can see. Then I'll have a better idea of what is there and we can figure out what we can do.*

At the livery stable, he saw old Jim Moore, owner of the stable, and he and Jim talked for a little bit. He found a pretty good saddle horse. Jim said, "What are you going to be doing with yourself here for a while, Clint?"

Clint said, "Gee, I don't know. I've just come back and I've gotta figure out something so I can get settled down."

"Well, why don't you come down and work for me at the stable here? We're not too busy anymore, but we still have folks coming in with their wagons and their teams, and there are still some people coming in from outside wanting to rent a buggy and a team. You know, there is still some country that doesn't have very good roads yet."

Clint said, "Well, I'll give that a long thought. That's a good idea."

Clint got on his horse and rode north out of town, following the valley. As he covered the miles, he could see all of the new homes: there were no more "soddies" anymore, but homes with nice barns and outbuildings. It was a little early for them to be starting their spring planting, yet the cattle yards seemed to be full, as well as the hog yards. There seemed to be plenty of grain out in the granaries. He went on up toward the end of the Logan Valley, and there it was: about 120 acres of prairie, never touched, still Indian land and never opened for lease. Next to it was a small house and some barns on an 80-acre plot. He could envision all of that put together. If he could just find out the status of this final land and make a deal, he could combine it and then get himself into the kind of farming that he knew about, that he had learned in his work with Careyhurst. It would fulfill his lifelong ambition, and, more importantly, it would be with Carrie.

He stopped by to visit one of his old friends, a neighbor who had already secured his piece of the Indian land. Now, with his new family and a couple of years of farming in, he was doing very well. He and Mr. Hegwer talked for a while. Mrs. Hegwer invited him for lunch; they had a great time. Shortly after noon, about one-thirty or so, he said, "Well, I've got to get back. I'm going to be seeing Carrie again this evening."

They said, "Oh! Tell her hello for us. We know that if the two of you get back together again, you're going to do very well."

Riding back to Pender, Clint was thinking about how he could learn when and if this land was going to be opened up by the agency over in Winnebago. He remembered his sister, Fanny, and her husband, Ben Friese, and that Ben was a very successful farmland sales/broker/investor in mortgages. They might still be living in Pender. He hadn't seen Fanny in many, many years, but now he decided that he must see her and Ben. And then he must sit down with Carrie and discuss with her what he was dreaming of, what would make all things possible. At his first opportunity, he must ask Carrie for her hand in marriage.

Clint noted that it was getting a little late. The sun was coming down, and he was going to have to hurry up to get back to the livery stable and get cleaned up for dinner at Carrie's house.

He got to Carrie's house just as dinner started.

"Gee, Clint, where have you been all day?" said Carrie. "I saved a place for you. We'll have some dinner and then we can talk about everything."

About eight, after dinner was done and the dishes had been washed and put away, Clint and Carrie sat down in the living room and Clint said, "I've been up north to the north end of the Logan Valley, to that land that we've talked about, and it's still there. That's where we should be. Carrie, I want you to marry me, and I want us to get back to our life as we had planned, and we will do so well. I love you so much. Carrie, what do you say?"

Carrie said, "Clint, you know how much I love you."

Clint said, "Well, Carrie, I haven't told you, but you are so beautiful. Let's make our plans."

She said, "Yes. Let's do that."

Clint said, "The first thing I'm going to do tomorrow is see Ben Friese, Fanny's husband—you know Ben."

She said, "Sure I do."

"Well, I'm going to find out if he can be of help to us, and we then can talk about how we can put things together. Now, I've got a little cash that I saved from Wyoming, and perhaps you'll have a little bit, from your house and the like. Let's see what we can put together, and then we can make some real plans. I'm going to go back to the hotel and get some things together. I'll see you tomorrow." Clint took Carrie in his arms and said, "This is forever, Carrie."

She said, "Yes, Clint. Forever."

Clint was so happy, back in his hotel room, making notes about plans that he knew he could make come true.

The next morning he went to the hotel dining room for breakfast. He sat in a booth by himself, enjoying the rich, black coffee and reading over his notes of how his plans were beginning to take shape. The décor of the dining room had not changed in all the years he had known the place: the booths were very dark wood and showed the wear of the thousands of patrons who had sat in them over the decades. Truth was, they weren't even particularly comfortable, but they were familiar. This was home.

Then he heard voices behind him as three or four men climbed into the booth behind his, joking with each other and jostling his seat more than what should have been necessary. Clint grimaced. This probably meant he would be leaving soon, because there was no way he could think with loud voices so close behind him. But then he recognized one of the voices: it was Mr. Mahoney, Marie's father.

Clint already knew that Mr. Mahoney was a wealthy land investor and a commercial building contractor, certainly a prominent businessman in Pender; in fact, in the whole state of Nebraska. It soon became clear that the breakfast meeting was actually a business meeting among friends. Clint listened for a time but he couldn't determine who the other men were, and he finally felt that he shouldn't be eavesdropping on their conversation. He started preparing to leave. But then the talk behind him took a personal turn when one of the men asked about Mahoney's older daughter.

"How is your daughter Mary doing, Jim?" a man asked. "She still teaching music at that university?"

"Oh, yes. Doing well," said Mr. Mahoney. "Mary always manages to do well. Could always count on her. Her mother and

I—before she died—had already given up on Mary getting married, though."

The other men murmured in acknowledgment. One said, "I guess that happens sometimes when these smart young women get so educated. But at least Mary can make her own money—that's good if she's not going to get paired up with a husband."

"You hear from her right along, though, don't you?" asked another man at the table.

"Yes, yes. I get letters regularly from Mary. She tries harder to write since her mother's been gone. Looking out for me, I guess." For a moment the men at the table were silent, then Jim Mahoney continued, "Now the younger one, Marie ... I just have no idea. Haven't heard from her in a long time."

Clint sat so still he was barely breathing.

"Nothing like her sister," said Marie's father. "We failed her somehow, her mother and I did. We must have, or she wouldn't have turned out like this. I wish I at least knew where she is."

There was just no denying the pain that had hit Clint in the chest when the talk started up about Marie. For a second, a tiny flare of hope sprang up that he might learn where she had gotten to, but that was immediately snuffed out. Clint grabbed his things and left the hotel dining room. *Bad enough to have my own grief without her father's too!*

Later that morning, he got to a phone and called Fanny. After talking with her a little bit, he asked about Ben, and she got Ben to come to the phone. Ben said, "Well, Clint, come on up to the house. I've got my office here in the house now. We can sit down and talk this over and see what is possible."

Clint said, "I'll be right there." He walked through town and up to Ben's home, which was high on the hill where all the town's very fine homes were.

Ben welcomed him in and said, "Come on in and sit down, Clint. Tell me what you have in mind."

So, Clint outlined to him how he was seeing things: the plot of prairie and the 80 acres next to it, privately owned, and then the private, Indian-lease land nearby. He said, "If we could work this, we could get 200 to 240 acres. The prairie is about 80 acres, and it would be right next to the 80-acre home place. The outbuildings are sufficient. They're not much; the house isn't much, but it is sufficient to get started."

Ben said, "Let me look into it here. I'll be checking with the agency; I'll see the surveys. Let's see what their schedule is. Meanwhile, I understand you and Carrie are going to be married. Now, you've been in Wyoming most of the past ten years. What's been holding you up?"

"Well, it's a long story, Ben, but I had a great life at Careyhurst."

"Yes," he said, "I know the Careys through my work in land trading, land values, and some of my ranch land that I deal with—not in Wyoming, but down mostly in Oklahoma. And I know about the Careys buying and selling cattle from the different ranches. They are fine people, and you were with a very good ranch company in Careyhurst. Bob is a great man. I understand he's the governor now. He's going to be a senator soon, I think."

Clint said, "Yes, I think so."

Finally Ben got to his feet and said, "Well, Clint, I'll get started on this and be in touch as soon as I have anything to share with you. Now, you and Carrie keep in touch with me too. Let's get together sometime—Fanny and myself, you and Carrie— and get some plans made."

Clint went back to the livery stable. There was not much going on. He made some more notes of his plans, and he got to thinking about things. Marie hadn't come into his mind in quite some time, but hearing her father talk about her had brought it all back—painfully. He shook his head as if to get the painful memories shaken out. *It's not likely she ever will come back, and it's just as well. I'm headed off in a new direction now, and my plans don't include Marie.* He thought about that a moment. *No, my life doesn't include Marie now; that's all over with. It's done for.* He began to think about his new responsibilities, with Carrie and her son and daughter. *They will be my new family; I'm sure Carrie has thought about it too.* He wasn't concerned about what happened in her previous marriage; that was all while he was in Wyoming and he was not a part of it. She had made her own life then, and now they would make their life together, as they had originally planned.

Two months after Clint's return to Pender, a letter arrived from the Office of the Governor, State of Wyoming. It was addressed simply to: "Clinton Morgan, Pender, Nebraska." Clint wondered what Bob Carey could possibly want from him at this point. He opened the envelope and found a very short note, which read:

> *Dear Clint:*
> *I'm so sorry about the sale of the cattle. I know now what happened.*
> *I wish you the best of everything.*
> *Your friend,*
> *Bob*

Well, Clint thought. *So Bob somehow learned the truth of what happened there, that I was not part of that ill-conceived sale of the Herefords; he should have known that I would never have done anything that stupid.* He wondered briefly if it had really been necessary for him to resign so suddenly. Surely it would have all sorted itself out without his having to leave. *Well, truth is, it was probably about time for me to be leaving Careyhurst anyway. It was just unfortunate that it was under a cloud not of my making.* Clint noticed a strange thing then: a kind of warmth had come into his chest for Careyhurst, for Bob, for the memories of all he had learned there, and now, for the fact that Bob had clearly come to see that there hadn't really been anything to forgive. *Things have a way of working out.*

Still, it made a difference to him. As the days went on in the summer, Clint had a lighter heart with no longer any bad memories of Wyoming, as he and Carrie made their wedding plans for early fall 1923.

Wesley had been elected Thurston County sheriff. His ultimate goal, through his law study, was to become an attorney for the county and the area. The sheriff's job in Thurston County was a very important one because of the law enforcement with the two Indian tribes, the Omahas and the Winnebagos, and it was a new country, a new land. There were many challenges not met in some of the more settled parts of Nebraska. So, Wes was very busy in his new life. He and Irene were expecting their first child, and to them was a daughter born.

Fanny and Ben Friese, and Carrie and Clint had many meetings and dinners together and the plans developed.

That fall, Clint took Duncan up on his offer and went out to the Laird farms. He helped with the harvest, working mainly in the corn harvest. It wasn't so much for the income, though he made a few dollars; he wasn't concerned about that but it was something to keep him busy and to get a good observation of how things were going, what the prices were for corn, cattle, and hogs. He got himself informed on all of that. He was also looking into what he would need in terms of machinery. He intended to farm with horses, no mechanization. Even though he saw that some of the farmers in the area were moving in that direction on their farmlands, it still wasn't, in his opinion, very efficient in its operation. His plan seemed to be the most economical. Farm labor was cheap. Good young men could be found just by providing a place for them and their keep. Pay was maybe twenty dollars a month, maybe a little more during harvest with a bonus. He knew that he could put that together and make things come out profitably.

Finally one day Ben Friese called. He said, "Clint, I think I've got something here that you really should consider. It's going to be possibly another year, even maybe two years before we can get this put together with the Winnebago land leases and the lease of the 120-acre home place. Meanwhile, I've got a small place down south of Omaha along the Platte River. It's about 120 acres and it's going to be available right after January 1. If you and Carrie could get everything put together, we could get you up there and get you started. It's a nice little place, and I think that you ought to give it some serious consideration. You let me know, now."

Clint said, "Well, thanks, Ben. I'll get back to you as quick as I can. Carrie and I are going to see how we can make everything come together here."

This was now early November, after the harvest at Duncan Laird's farm. He and Carrie decided that they had better set a wedding date and plan a short honeymoon down to Omaha and over to see the place Ben was talking about. Carrie was very interested and said she wanted to see how they could put it together.

The wedding was planned for December. It would be just a small wedding at the house with Wes and Irene, with Wes being best man. Then the two of them would have someone watch the home and Ardell and Clarabelle, and they would take a few days and get on down to Omaha.

When they got to Omaha, Clint rented a one-horse shay. They went on out to the little community of LaPlatte, near South

Omaha, and then on to this little farm Ben had described—and there they found a beautiful, large home with brick and stone walls, two stories. The bottom story was one big, open kitchen/dining room/living area. Outside were the stairs up to the rooms. This was their farmhouse but it had once been an inn of the Butterfield Stage Lines. It was the Platte River Trail and the last stop for Butterfield on its way to Omaha.

A memory came into Clint's mind of when, as a much younger man, he had ridden the Butterfield stagecoach to El Dorado to go to work in the oilfields and nearly lost his Lucchese boots to a thief in the night.

Now, he and Carrie looked everything over and quickly decided that this was the place to begin their life together. He got back with Ben Friese, and then he and Carrie put together all their finances. Carrie put her place up for sale, and Clint got busy getting machinery and livestock. It turned out that the small farm was owned by Ben, so there was no lease fee. Whatever Clint had, if they had a crop, it would have some profit.

Right after January 1, Carrie's house had sold. They were doing pretty well. The two of them together had about $5,000. They were very careful and were able to get all of the necessary things together for their household and then get everything moved.

1924 was their first year together, farming the land on this beautiful hillside farm. Down from the stately old inn, now converted to a wonderful family home, was a running stream and a stone bridge, right on down to the Platte River. Ardell was old enough to be of some help in the farm work, but polio had done enough damage to his legs that Clint gave him only small, regular chores; it looked certain that Ardell would never make a real farmhand. He and the boy had become friends, though, and got along well, after Clint's initial adjustment of learning to live in a household with children. Clarabelle, of course, was devoted to her mother and was her mother's primary helper.

They had a very good crop. Carrie also had income from the produce of the chickens and the milk cows, so they had cash.

In February 1925 a son was born to them, and Clint was so happy. They named the baby Frank. Clint and Carrie, in their love, just knew that everything was going to turn out the best that either of them could ever have imagined. But, in fact, the addition of their own son opened an unexpected rift between Clint and Ardell. The boy had been accustomed to having the majority of his mother's attention, especially during the worst of the polio. With the coming of the new baby, Ardell felt left out and blamed Clint. Unfortunately, Clint was too busy to notice that trouble had taken root in his relationship with his stepson. By contrast, Clarabelle was delighted with her new baby brother.

Later in the year 1925, Ben got in touch with them. He said, "It's getting near the time now. We've got to get back up to the Winnebago agency and get our bids in and see if we can get the lease lands. It takes some time to get the Indian family signatures on the leases, so we need to get that taken care of in order to be ready for the spring farming of 1926."

Once the leases were finally signed by all the necessary parties, Clint and Carrie had to organize to move from the Butterfield Stage Lines farmhouse to their new farm. Clint's attention was consumed with the relocation. Transporting everything required two railroad cars, not counting the livestock. First Clint loaded everything up in Omaha and then went on down to Thurston. There they unloaded household goods and machinery, and got it all moved out to the new farm.

Clint almost forgot about getting his things from the hotel that Mrs. Smith had saved for him, so on the way up in the move, he stopped by and picked up everything. He talked with her, settled up with her, and took a bit of time to go through some of his possessions. He hadn't thought much about what his life had been the past fifteen years.

Then he saw among his things the only remembrance he had of his father, which was a small tintype picture of his father and two business assistants, obviously taken in a saloon in their typical Western wear. That he treasured. He had learned that Chauncy, his father, had passed away in early 1922. He did not know where.

The lantern was there too. But he refused to dwell on the memory of the night he had taken Marie from Rosie's to live at Careyhurst.

He also often had some memory, which would never completely leave him, of the shooting in the terrible incident after the vaudeville show in the Opera House. Thoughts of Marie still came—just now and then; not so much anymore. He hoped that, wherever she was, she was doing well and was taken care of. She would always have a part of his heart, but at this time, not a part of his life.

Clint and Carrie settled into the new place. The home was very modest, hardly large enough. There was a separate, small building that was converted to a bunkhouse, a place to house the men that he hired to work full time in the fields. They had to get started. It was a mild winter, so they all were ready to go early in March. Clint had accumulated enough farm equipment. Ben had helped him out on securing some extra cash for working money for seeds, grain and hay for the livestock, and enough to start out with the necessary brood sows for the hog-raising, so that they could get under way. Carrie got Clarabelle and Ardell started in the nearby, brand new country schoolhouse, less than a mile away. It felt like a new country. Clarabelle continued to do very well in the new school—unlike Ardell, who took an immediate dislike to the teacher. More than once, Clint had to leave off his work opening the new fields to see about the trouble Ardell was having in school.

The first of the fields Clint opened was on the 80-acre plot of prairie, turning that sod to its first year of production. As the men went to the field with their sulky plows, each pulled by a team of two horses, what a wonderful, magic view of the sulkys turning the black sod, as if creating ribbons of velvet on the verdant green of the prairie. All of those fields were turned. One small field of the lease land was prepared to raise small grain, oats, so that they would have plenty of grain for feed for the livestock. There would be, the first year, well over one hundred acres of corn, and as they went on through this first year, the rains were good, the soil was so rich, and at harvest time, they were harvesting corn at near one hundred bushels per acre—almost unheard of. So, the total harvest, less his expense and paying the cornhuskers and getting the grain to market, put him in a very solid cash position. He also, for the remaining prairie field, secured hay balers, and they had a very fine crop of baled hay.

So, this first year looked very successful, and the good fortune continued on into the next year. By 1928, Carrie and Clint were among the most successful in the Logan Valley farming. Ardell had, all on his own, discovered the outdoors and had begun spending his days traipsing through the flat farm land, over the hills, down into the ravines. His legs grew steadily stronger, overcoming at last most of the effects of the polio. The year he turned thirteen, he found himself—to his own amazement—to be among the more athletic of the boys in his school.

When Carrie's son Frank was three, she took him with her on the train to Omaha, where she went shopping and outfitted herself in the ladies-wear section of the Brandeis Department

Store. She visited her sister, who lived in Omaha. While in the city, she went boldly to the Ford dealer and bought—paying cash—a brand-new Model A four-door sedan and drove it home, with young Frank sitting in the passenger seat, content even though he could see only sky through the windows.

At first Clint was perfectly happy to ignore his wife's Ford and get around with his shay. But the day came when Clint had to learn to drive, and Carrie helped him. He then became a great fancier of the new automobile, though never one for the mechanization of farming with tractors or the like. He just didn't care for that.

The new automobile made it possible for them to get easily back and forth to shopping, to their social activities, to the bank, Carrie to her church, Clint to travel quickly to the Indian agency to get leases renewed. It was a great thing for them.

Clint had learned much of his management skills and approach at Careyhurst, and he was never one to do any more than necessary in working the fields. He had his hired men; he supervised that work and was able to look at each phase of the farm production. In that manner, he made the farm more profitable than if he had not paid for extra help but had tried to do all of the work himself, neglecting the real management duties of his farming operation. This practice helped to make him a respected leader.

Along with his success managing his farm, Clint also managed at last to bring into his life the intellectual stimulation he had long wished for. He still reviewed his weathered copy of *Self-Reliance*, but he hungered for the give-and-take of political conversation with other minds of both agreeing and opposing viewpoints. He began to convene dinners during the fall harvest, bringing in his own choice of guests, usually six or eight at each dinner. Sometimes he even hired certain men to work the harvest less for their skill as harvesters and more for their ability to hold their own in intellectual conversation. Of course, Carrie's years running a boarding house had equipped her well to prepare and serve such dinners for many guests.

One of Clint's favorite guests was John Dillon, who always arrived in his Ford with a supply of *Daily Worker* newspapers and other communist writings. Dillon was from an Eastern family. As an avowed socialist, he brought balance to the discussions at the dinners, which were generally all-male events until Miss Lowell, a local schoolteacher, won a place at the table by proving herself knowledgeable about history and the political stances of the incoming Roosevelt Administration. All of Clint's guests could and did speak fluently and authoritatively to their individual political leanings. One or two might recite relevant poetry. It was an honor to be invited to the dinners, and anyone who did not contribute to the conversation was not invited to return—though if the man was hired to be a harvester, he did not lose that position.

The landowner John Haskell and the local district congressman were among regular dinner guests. Clint generally opened the evening by introducing each person present, then recounting an adventure or two from his Wyoming days before moving the talk toward political events of the day. The dinners were always lively and often continued until eight-thirty in the evening.

Clint's own political views tended to be quite liberal. He became a profound influence in the community, often advising the County Board of Supervisors and helping to elect county judges. In the coming years, he would be aligned philosophically with Roosevelt's efforts to help the plight of farmers.

The dinners continued from 1929 into the early 1930s when Clint was doing well with the farm. He and Carrie were living well. When their youngest, Frank, started school, he was thrilled to recognize Miss Lowell, his teacher, as one of the people who had come to his father's dinners, and Clint highly approved of someone of her caliber being in charge of his son's early education. "You listen to her," Clint told Frank. "She knows what she's talking about."

Clint and Carrie's life had by this time taken on a settled and almost majestic bearing. The farm had proven very profitable, and all three children were doing well. But almost imperceptibly, things had already begun to change.

Adversity is like a strong wind.
It tears away from us all but the things that cannot be torn, so
that we see ourselves as we really are
— Arthur Golden

CHAPTER 6
CLINT MEETS HIS DESTINY

It wasn't so noticeable at first—just that farm prices were not quite so good. Clint had no way of realizing what was ahead: the collapse of the farm economy with the deepening of the Great Depression.

To please Carrie and also to make it better for himself, he found about a mile up the hill above the lowlands a farm coming available for lease with outbuildings and a beautiful three-bedroom home. He wanted that for Carrie: to have a nice home, which she had not had in their very small place, though she had made the best of things. But now she would have this fine home, and Clint would have the barns and other buildings. He made the agreement for the farm with the man who had become his lifelong friend, John Haskell.

Mr. Haskell was a large landowner of many farms and he never dealt much with banks. He dealt directly with the insurance companies in financing. For this particular farm, Mr. Haskell had a very favorable lease arrangement on sharing a bit of the farm crop production and then Clint invested in some new buildings, one particularly for his hog-raising operation. He also lined up some remodeling of the home. He unwittingly depreciated his cash balance, and his crops of 1932 and '33 became, in the Crash, practically worthless: corn prices at five and ten cents a bushel, not enough money to pay for their harvest.

Despite this severe setback, Clint kept going; there seemed little else he could do. He drove to the Winnebago agency, as he had done every year, to renew his leases. By 1933, he had accumulated four separate parcels of 40 acres each and one of 30 acres. But when he attempted to renew the lease on the 30-acre parcel, he learned that he had been outbid.

"What?!" said Clint. "Who outbid me?"

"Herman Schmidt," said the agent. "Know 'im?"

Of course Clint knew him. He had talked with Schmidt just a matter of a few months earlier. He was a real estate broker in Pender. Schmidt had told Clint that the Indian agency was planning to open lands along the Missouri River for lease. Clint remembered the conversation because he had hoped the new lease land would be rich lands along the river, but it turned out to be hill country marked by a deep ravine.

Clint was infuriated that Herman Schmidt had taken his leased parcel right out from under him before he could get it renewed. He left the agency in a rage. *I just bet I know where to find him.*

Clint drove by the Pender saloon, found Herman Schmidt's car parked in front, and went into the saloon. Once inside, he ordered a drink at the bar and took it to the table where Schmidt was seated. "Herman, we need to talk."

Looking up, Schmidt's eyes widened a bit when he saw who was addressing him. Clint didn't wait for an answer or an invitation. He sat down, took a drink, and turned a fierce eye on Schmidt.

"Herman, I just found out that you outbid me on a parcel of land I've been leasing. Want to tell me about that?"

Schmidt said nothing but finished his drink. Clint went on.

"Now, I know you've done this before—you grab a lease that's almost up for renewal, then you turn around and sublease or share-crop the land. Isn't that right? That's what you've been doing, Herman?"

There was still no answer from the real estate broker.

"Well, you're not going to do that to me." Clint took his wallet out of an inside coat pocket, opened it, and withdrew a blank bank check. He laid the bank check on the table and returned his hands to his lap.

Schmidt started to get up.

Quietly and coldly Clint said, "Herman, I'd advise you not to get up. My .38 is pointed right between your legs. If I have to use it, you'll be left without the ability to do much good with those young German girls anymore."

Schmidt turned as white as the shirt he was wearing. He gave up the idea of leaving the table.

Clint went on. "The sheriff and his deputies are sitting over there, just a few tables behind your left shoulder. He already knows what we're discussing. The agency is knowledgeable about it too. Now, here's what we're going to do." He nodded his head toward the bank check. "You're going to write in today's date and make the check out to cash, and then sign it. Then we're going to get up, go outside together, and walk up to the bank. You're going to go up to the teller and find out how much you have on deposit, just to make sure your account can cover our transaction."

Schmidt stared unblinking at Clint.

"Let's get going, nice and easy," said Clint. "I'll carry the check and the .38."

The bank was just two doors up from the saloon. It turned out that Herman Schmidt's account had just over five thousand dollars in it. The teller had written the amount on a slip of paper, which Schmidt showed to Clint.

Clint nodded. "Now, I figure that 30-acre parcel is worth around three thousand dollars, but, tell you what, we're going to round that up to four thousand dollars. You write that in on the check."

Despite looking as though he might faint at any moment, Schmidt wrote the amount in, first in numbers, then in words, in a surprisingly steady hand.

"Now you go back up to the teller, and get the four thousand dollars."

Moments later Schmidt stepped away from the teller's window, and Clint instructed him to go to his car. Clint walked beside him. Once inside the vehicle, Clint said, "Okay, Herman, hand me the cash." Money in hand, Clint continued, "Now, here's your new situation, Herman. You're out of business in Thurston County. I'll give you twenty-four hours to get out of town."

Clint stepped out of the car. Herman started the engine, backed out, and drove away. Likely as not, Schmidt figured he had got off easy.

Even with the transfusion of the money from the lost lease parcel, life for Clint and Carrie became a matter of trying to figure out how they were going to make it through the next year. Things did not get better. They got exceedingly worse. Starting in 1934 was the tragedy of the drought, along with bad weather and hailstorms that literally destroyed the corn crop.

Little known to Clint, this devastating year, 1934, was also the year that his friend Mrs. Carey passed away at the age of seventy-seven. She had lived ten years as a widow after Joseph Maull Carey died in 1924 at the age of seventy-nine.

Clint and Carrie, in the early 1930s, were proud of Ardell and Clarabelle. Ardell had by this time become a notable athlete. He had continued to immerse himself in high school sports, and in 1933 and 1934, he was the quarterback who led his high school football team to two undefeated seasons. He had also become a skilled lightweight boxer. Clint admired Ardell's success in boxing, which was something he understood, and the two were bonded by boxing for the rest of their lives.

Meanwhile, Clarabelle had graduated from high school, where she had been an excellent student. Contrary to Carrie's wishes, Clarabelle did not marry and start a family, but chose to enroll in a teacher's college to prepare to teach in a rural school.

As the 1930s progressed, most all of the farms were in very bad condition. In many situations, the farmers lost their farms to the bankers. The bankers would try to keep them on as sharecroppers; fortunately, that didn't happen for Clint because John Haskell stayed with him, and that became the one saving grace, enabling Clint to stay on his farm. He managed to keep two of the most valuable Indian land leases and, by 1936, was hopeful that he would persevere until the drought conditions and the economy took a turn for the better.

Clint turned again and again to his worn, cloth-bound copy of *Self-Reliance* until one day he realized that he had memorized the opening poem and no longer had to open the pages to access it. He quoted it to himself as he considered the bank statements, walked the parched land, and thought of how best to deal with his starving livestock:

"Ne te quaesiveris extra"
[Do not seek for things outside of yourself]

Man is his own star; and the soul that can
Render an honest and a perfect man,
Commands all light, all influence, all fate;
Nothing to him falls early or too late.
Our acts our angels are, or good or ill,
Our fatal shadows that walk by us still.

Sometimes when the words of the poem sat in his heart, he would wonder why he had never made it to college. He knew he was smart enough and would probably have done very well. What was it that had misdirected his life? He thought about how his first job had been as a bar boy, then his father had urged him to go on the Trek West—just him, not his brothers. There was no one to mentor him to go in a different direction, even though his interest in reading was already apparent. Then there was Marie and the Dodge City Opera House, where he had killed a man. *That was it*, he realized. His life had changed forever when he killed Fredrik. How hard he had tried to run from that, to hide his identity, to conceal who he really was. So many doors had suddenly felt closed to him. The only doors that opened were the ones leading to his life in farming. *And that led to this dry wasteland I'm staring at now.*

Unfortunately, 1936 doubled up into another year of drought. There was absolutely no crop. There was no rain from March to October of that year. Clint was completely out of hay and grain and feed. It was very, very difficult. He had no more credit at the bank; he had no other resources; he had no one. Even those neighboring farmers whom he had helped in the past and still had some means would not even consider signing a note with him for funds. He did, however, go into the new Farm Home Administration Office and make application for a grant that would help him get restarted. Some of the farmers who had qualified and already received help the previous year had survived. Some who were in locations where there had been some rain and had some crop had done reasonably well.

But the Farm Home Administration Office was slow to respond to Clint and he was losing hope. He was worried that he wouldn't even be able to renew the leases on his Indian land.

As September of 1936 neared, he had some very hard decisions to make. He and Carrie talked about it, trying to determine how they could possibly stay and make it through. They could not come up with anything.

Then, the Wednesday after Labor Day, it was a hot, dry day with a gusty wind blowing tumbleweeds and dust across the road from the field in which nothing grew, and it blew right across into the farmyard. Clint was sitting in a shaded area on one side of the barn, waiting for nothing, wondering what tomorrow might bring, when he heard the sound of a car coming from over the hill. In those days, an automobile on the road, except for the mailman, was a great occasion. He got up and waited for the car to come down the hill. The car came down slowly, then turned into the driveway. It was a new 1936 black, four-door, Ford sedan. It came into the driveway and stopped. Clint walked over to the car. The passenger door opened and out came John Haskell. He said, "Good afternoon, Clint. She's a warm one, isn't she?"

Clint said, "Yes, it's been this way for most of the summer and, as you can see, things are not so good, John."

"I know, Clint. I brought some men here who want to speak to you. I think you'll be interested in hearing what they have to say. Oh, my driver here, he is my business manager; I don't know whether you've ever met him. He's William Smith. Been with me a long time now. I don't drive so much anymore and he helps me out a lot. Now, you fellows in back, come on out here and meet Clint."

Out of the back seat came two men dressed in black suits and ties.

"Clint, I want you to meet Jim Phillips. Jim is an FBI agent and he'll be talking to you. And then his associate here is Tom Rosenfeldt. Tom is a special agent with the United States Secret Service. Let's get over here in the shade a little bit. I'd like to stay outside here and not go to the house, if you don't mind. This is rather confidential. They have something they'd like to talk to you about and ask your help, and I think you will be interested. I know them, I trust them. Now, Jim and Tom, you two tell Clint what you are here today to outline to him, what you would like to have him help you with in your mission."

Jim turned to Clint and said, "Clint, we are on a very secret mission. We are concerned about the infiltration of German agents representing Hitler and his group of stooges— Goebbles, for one. We have one man in particular who is one of their top agents, and we have been tracing him and his activities. We've learned something of great interest and we are sure that there is soon to be a culmination of this one particular man's mission. Tom, tell him a little of your part in this."

Tom said, "Well, the Secret Service, as you probably know, has agents in Germany as well as in many other parts of the world. I work directly with a lot of them. The particular man we're talking about is a German agent we have been tracking both in Germany and in his activities here in the United States. Now, you're probably wondering why he would be here in this part of Nebraska."

Jim broke in, "Clint, the man we're speaking of is Hans von Essen. Now, I think you know who he is. He's the man who was involved with Marie Mahoney even in the years when you knew and were close to Marie. We also know, Clint, that you are the one who shot his brother at the vaudeville show at the Dodge City Opera House."

At the mention of Marie, Clint had tightened on the inside and slapped a defensive, impassive expression on his face, but the reference to the Opera House incident in which he had killed a man was such a shock that he had to look away.

Jim Phillips went right on speaking as though he hadn't noticed, but Clint knew that he had. "That, then, takes us to Hans and his life with Marie. Now, we know that you lost contact with Marie after you were in France and she was no longer at Careyhurst, and that you have no record of what happened to her and where she is."

Is there anything about my personal life you fellas don't know?! Irritation was taking center stage in Clint's emotions but he held it in check because he sensed that he was about to learn, at last, where Marie had gone.

Jim continued: "I'll tell you that she is now living with Hans. From the time she left Careyhurst, she has been most of the time in San Francisco and has performed in various clubs and in many of the productions and the special shows. She has had a very close friend through the years whose name is Lily Lupino."

Well, that has to be a stage name!

"Now Lily is one of our agents also," said Jim, "and Lily is the one who has informed us of Marie, of Hans, and also of your history with Marie. We know that Marie and Hans purchased a large acreage that just recently came available over near the Missouri River, a remote area near the Winnebago agency."

It was all Clint could do to keep his jaw from dropping open. He knew that area! A picture of it formed in his mind as Jim continued.

"We believe Hans needed a very remote area because of his work with German intelligence. He needed to build a hidden facility to establish his shortwave radio stations, his presses, and all that he needs to bring in to strengthen his contacts with the other agents who will be filtering out through the United States, involved in sabotage and espionage, working undercover with the isolationist groups, the German American Bund." Jim paused and took a breath. "So, we need your help, Clint."

Despite his stream of thoughts in reaction to what he was hearing, Clint had listened without comment. Now he looked at both of the men and said, "Well, go on. What is it you want me to do to assist you?"

Jim and Tom looked at each other, then Jim said, "We need to keep our identities as undercover agents secret, but we have to get to the land that Hans and Marie have purchased. We need to have assistance from you to go there, survey the area, and report to us what is on site there. We cannot do that ourselves without revealing our undercover work. We know you can. We believe that you could arrange a meeting with Marie. You haven't seen her in a long time."

Clint listened but felt his eyes narrow just a bit. *See Marie again?* A strange mix of emotions surged into his heart.

"Now, at the moment Hans is in Germany. He makes trips back and forth. He is over there working with Goebbles and his men on the propaganda plan. He's met with German engineers on equipping shortwave radio stations, and he is already training agents under his supervision who will work closely with him here in the United States."

Clint learned that after Hans had buried Fredrik's body in Germany in 1913, he had come back to the United States. Through the years, Hans was with Marie and Lily with occasional trips back to Germany. He was on one of those trips to his homeland in 1917 when Clint rescued Marie from Rosie's bordello. At some point after that, when Clint was in France during the war, Hans again returned to America and met up with Marie, who left Careyhurst and abandoned any plans of a life with Clint. From then on, Marie was performing with Lily or traveling with Hans until 1933, when Marie and Hans acquired the land. Along the way, Hans had fallen in with the Social Nazi movement. Many of his friends in the entertainment business were already involved. Goebbles was particularly taken with Hans because of his frequent trips to America and his knowledge of show business and of the large first-generation German communities in the United States.

"Goebbles pegged Hans as somebody who might be able to carry through the Nazi plans to influence the isolationist movement to interfere with Roosevelt's effort to help England and rearm America," said Jim.

"Well, that wasn't all," said Tom. "Hans was also spending a lot of time, when he was in Germany, with the heroes of the Luftwaft." His words came out hard with sarcasm. "He even met Charles Lindbergh, who was in Germany ostensibly to sell aircraft but in fact he was helping Germany build its Luftwaft in preparation for aerial warfare."

"Anyway," Jim said, "Hans is an important pawn in Goebbles' master propaganda and espionage plan. Then on one of his trips back to America, he joined a vaudeville show in San Francisco with his acrobatic act and met up with Marie again." Jim stopped talking to glance through some papers, apparently to make sure he had given Clint the most important details. "Oh," he added. "One more thing by way of background: I want to tell you, too, that Hans got married in Germany some years back. He has a wife there and has a family with her."

Oh, Marie, did you have any idea what you were getting yourself into?

"Now, we would like to have you visit Marie and then survey the area, give us specifics of how it is laid out, the buildings that are there. From Lily, we learned that they have a nice new home; there is one building that has some brand-new farm equipment. Apparently, the cover is to establish a working farm. Lily has visited Marie there and she knows that there is a building that is going up in a concealed area, and so we need to get information on all of this. At some point, we are going to confront Hans and all who are involved with him in what we believe will be an important revelation of Germany's undercover activities here in the United States. Germany is involved in efforts to heighten the isolationist activity of this country, to slow down any attempt to get funds for our government to build our aircraft industry, and to reveal details about materials and aircraft going to help the British."

Finally Clint spoke: "Tell me more about Lily Lupino."

Jim said, "Lily Lupino has long been associated with Marie. Her background is that she was a performer—and still is—both a dancer and, frankly, sometimes a stripper with some of the burlesque and traveling vaudeville groups. She is also a very astute, well-educated agent of ours. She's worked with us for many years. She's been able to identify a number of people, many with some allegiance in show business and some of the more famous names, not the least of which is Charles Lindbergh, who we know—as Tom was mentioning—has been working in Germany assisting the building of Hitler's air force."

Lily Lupino's involvement with the Secret Service began to make sense for Clint when he learned that she was the daughter of a high-level member of the US State Department's Foreign Service Office. Her real name was Agatha Aldrich, and she had grown up traveling the world with her parents as her father conducted management responsibilities for the budgets of US embassies in a number of different countries. She was well educated and spoke several languages fluently, notably German, Italian, and French, with a smattering of Chinese and Japanese as well. Her poise in the cosmopolitan arena was invaluable to the Secret Service. But from a young age, she had shown tremendous independence and unwillingness to restrict herself to the confines of the young woman her parents wanted her to be. Her early interest in dancing skewed into burlesque, then fan dancing, and ultimately she polished a two-sided career in legitimate stage as well as ribald and geek entertainment. But she never lost the business sense she inherited from her father, and she had always taken care of Marie.

Jim finished up his description of Lily's background with a short silence. Then he said, "Now, tell us, Clint. Can you help us?"

Clint said, "Well, I have to think about it a bit. Just exactly what is it and when do you need these things? I have some very difficult problems, not knowing what's going to happen here. Mr. Haskell, you know that I'll not be able to do anything as far as paying you for the use of this land this year. I'm not even sure I'll be able to survive here for another year. Things are very, very difficult for me."

Jim said, "Clint, you needn't worry. This is an opportunity for you. It's very dangerous, but I will tell you, you will be well compensated. We trust you. We know you are a brave man, very knowledgeable, with the ability to be involved in what we are doing, keeping total confidentiality."

Clint said, "Well, gentlemen, candidly, I don't have anything else to do, and I believe in what you are doing, and any way I can help, I will."

"Good!" said Jim. "Here's what we want. As soon as you can, you arrange to stop to see Marie. She's living there at the house. We'll give you a little bit about the location; I don't think you'll have any problem finding it from the roads off the

Winnebago Indian agency and then as the road goes across to the county seat in Pender. There is only one road in to it, and as you get there, you'll see the location and where the home is. As soon as you can, arrange a meeting with Marie to review old times, whatever you wish, and then take some time to look at the lay of the land. We believe that it's 500 acres or more, and it's located in a sloping, deep ravine."

Clint didn't divulge that he knew exactly where that land was.

"Some of it has never been used for any kind of farming purposes. It has not been occupied in many years. We want to know the location of the construction, the buildings. You needn't go in them, but just the location, the way that we can have access. Make your notes and bring them back to us.

"And then you will be contacted—not by us. You'll be contacted by Lily. We can tell you that Lily will be with a traveling show that is going to be in Pender sometime later this month. We would think about harvest time, maybe the first of October—you'll get the dates of when it's appearing. She's going to be with this traveling show, a small circus, and the sideshow. It's going to be Lily and her girls. You visit there. Lily will be able to locate you. You stop at the sideshow and you make contact with Lily, and she'll give you some information that will guide you. She'll give you a date and time when we plan to make our trip to the farm. We want to make it when we know that Hans will be there.

"Now, there's something you need to know. Hans knows that you are the one who shot and killed his brother. Lily told us that Marie told him about that. He has vowed to avenge his brother's death at some point. He's wanting to get to you. We don't think he's going to do anything right now, because his primary purpose is performing under orders from the Hitler people, but we would advise you to be very careful and be watchful. I don't know that he knows exactly where you are living, nor do I know that Marie knows, but she certainly knows something of the area, having grown up in the communities nearby. So, we warn you, no matter what, to be on your lookout.

"It's not just Hans alone you have to worry about. He has three men working with him, and you know he would be more likely to order one of them to take you out than kill you himself.

"Now, I think you need to have some expense money, and I think probably times are a little tough for you. Mr. Haskell, here, has an envelope that he'll give to you. You're going to find a nice little amount that should carry you for the next month or two for some of your expenses and some of your time. Then, as we get in touch with you, we'll be talking further. Do you have any questions?" He paused only a moment. "We're going to be on our way, and you can expect to hear from us soon, Clint."

Clint looked at both of them. "Gentlemen, I think I understand what you need." He shook hands with each of them.

Mr. Haskell handed him the envelope and said, "Clint, I must tell you also that Bob sends his regards. Now in his second term as senator of Wyoming, he remembers you well, thinks very highly of you. Because of his work with the committees, he is aware of the necessary undercover activities that we are doing to protect this country. We'll be seeing you soon, Clint. Have a nice day. Say 'Hello' to Carrie."

Clint shook hands with John then the driver started the Ford engine. They drove away, up the hill, and Clint walked on down to the house.

Without a word to Carrie, Clint retrieved his double-barreled shotgun from a back room, checked that it was loaded, and set it at the back door of the house, then he went throughout the house, making sure that every door and window was locked. He would keep his .38 beside him as he slept.

Carrie caught up with him as he finished securing the house. "What are you doing?" she asked. "Why are you locking everything up?"

"It's nothing to worry you. I got wind that there might be a gang moving through this area, folks who have had to resort to stealing because of the hard times. They're armed. I don't want them stealing anything from us on their way through."

Carrie seemed to accept his explanation. "Was that Mr. Haskell you were talking to?"

Clint said, "Yes, it was. He and some of his friends, business associates. They wanted to know how we are doing, and we talked for a little bit. I told him that I'd applied for a Farm Administration grant, and he said, 'Well, that's good. I want you to be able to stay here and hold on.' Then he advanced me a little bit to keep us going until the loan comes in. Carrie, I never expected anything like that."

Carrie said, "Oh my." She pointed at the envelope. "Let's see!"

"He just wants to help us out." Clint opened the envelope and counted out $200. That was more than they could have hoped for.

So, they went on into September, carefully handling the funds for what little they had left in the cows and the team of horses, a few chickens: buying feed and some hay and grain, and then some supplies for the kitchen. Carrie was able to get some flour and sugar, and the like. Things went with a little bit more hope. Clint said, "You know, Carrie, I think I can get the car running well enough, and I think I'd better get over to the agency and try to get those leases for another year. They know that there's no income from them, so nobody's going to be really that anxious, but I do want to get them secured. So, I think I'm going to look at the car a little bit. In the morning, I think I'll drive on over to Winnebago and see what I can do, then we can make some plans for the rest of the year."

Carrie said, "Well, okay."

Listening was his son, Frank, who said, "Hey, Dad, can I go with you tomorrow?"

"Well, I don't know, Son. You'd miss a day of school."

"Gee, I'd like to go. Can I go?"

Clint looked at Carrie, and Carrie said, "Yes, I think so."

Clint was reluctant, but he didn't want to give any hint that there was reason that his son should not go. "We'll leave early, now. We're probably going to leave around seven-thirty or eight, so you'll have to make sure you're ready."

Clint went out. The old Model A Ford was still running but not so great, and he did a few things with it, checked the tires and made sure the radiator had enough water. Fortunately, he had enough gas, and, of course, now he had a few dollars so he could get a fresh tankful of gas and some oil.

The next morning, he and son Frank went off to Winnebago. They got over there about nine-thirty. Clint went off into the reservation, on up along the river to bring in the owners of the parcels to the agency, where they met with the agency manager and succeeded in getting two leases renewed. One parcel was a little difficult in finding the owners and he wasn't sure he could handle it anyway, because of the supplies and horses and machinery required for it.

Finally about noon, Clint said, "Everybody, thanks so much. We'll be on our way. Let's hope for a good year, like the ones we used to have and not like this past year."

Clint and Frank drove on, cutting across country on a road that finally converged with the one main road that connected to the highway and close to home. They were out about ten miles and all of a sudden the car was not running well. It was obvious that something was wrong. As they ran down the hill a little bit, Clint saw to the right the driveway and a house. The engine had stopped; he let the car roll in there. He was sure that the radiator was low on water and the engine was overheated. So, there was nothing to do but let the car sit until it cooled. He and Frank got out and went up to the door and knocked. A nice lady came to the door. Clint looked up and it was Marie.

Marie said, "Oh my, Clint! It has been so many years! Come in! And is this your boy?"

"Yes, he is," said Clint.

"Well, young man, you come right on in here now. What brings you out this way?"

"Well," Clint said, "We've just been over to the agency to renew some leases. I don't know whether you know it or not, but that's where I have been all these years, over in the Logan Valley."

Marie said, "Come on in and we'll talk. Hans is not here. I don't know if you remember Hans. He's back in Germany now, but he's going to be back soon. He said he'd like to meet you."

It was obvious to Clint that, while she was still beautiful, she was wan, a little slow-moving, and not in the best of health.

She said, "Have you had any lunch?"

Clint said, "No, but we'll be all right. We'll be on our way as soon as I can get the radiator cool. If you get me to the well here, I'll get water for it."

Marie said, "Oh, we have running water. You don't have to look for the well. There's a bucket here. Let me help you. I'm going to fix a few things for you to eat. You just sit down."

"Well," Clint said, "I'll go get some water for the car first. Son, you sit down. I'm going to see to some things."

Marie went into another room and brought out some books and albums, and laid them out on a table. She said to Frank, "Here are some things you'd like to look at. It's all the things I did on stage, and there are pictures and stories." Then Marie went on to the kitchen and fixed ham sandwiches. She had a freshly baked apple pie and fresh milk. She fixed hot coffee.

Outside, Clint filled the radiator. In his pocket he carried a pencil and some notepaper. He looked around, took note of the home. Down adjacent to it was a large machine shed, and through a window, even from a distance, he could see a tractor and other brand-new farm equipment in the shed. On down from it, as the land looked towards the east and from north to south to the corner, was a deep ravine, which went on down into an area that would wind its way beyond to the last slope towards the river and the agency headquarters. But it was not passable by car; there were no roads. It was clearly an area that was very private, not noticeable from either side, and down towards the end was a low barnlike structure that could have been used for a garage or for livestock and the like. Then on to the north of the ravine was an area where he could see some new construction up on the hillside. Then across to the west the land was more level and, because of the lay of the slope, could be irrigated for crops. The acreage beyond that was pastureland. The house was very modern. In fact, it had electric lights; it had inside plumbing. Outside near the machine shed was an electric generator with powerlines from it on down to the other building. He carefully made his notes, estimating the perimeter of all of the area, the slope, the possible second entrance from one of the more distant roads to the fence line. This second entrance was not currently passable and would have to be approached through the ravine on foot or horseback.

Eventually, Clint came back into the house, and here was the wonderful luncheon Marie had been preparing.

"Let me just wash my hands before we eat," he said. In the bathroom, he found prescription bottles lined up on the counter. A pang went through him as he saw Maric's name on the labels.

They had their luncheon sandwiches and dessert. Marie said to Clint, "Come on into the living room. Frankie, you just keep looking around at those things."

Clint and Marie sat down in the living room and talked. She said, "Clint, it's been so long, and I'm so sorry, but it's the way things had to be. I just didn't feel that it was ever going to work out for the two of us at Careyhurst. I did leave and I went back to San Francisco." The expression on her face told him that her decisions had not come without regrets.

"I went down to Los Angeles for a while," Marie continued. "I worked in the clubs and some of the shows. I met my friend Lily Lupino. She's my best friend and we worked together. She worked in the shows. She did some special dancing and had her own entourage. Then later, Hans came back from Germany about 1932. He had developed his own acrobatic act and joined up with another traveling show. I got on there too, and we did quite well for a couple of years. Times got a little slow, as you know, and we haven't been doing much. He's been very busy with his estate and things in Germany. He will be back soon. He has some funds he's inherited and we're going to establish a little farm here for our retirement."

She spoke of Hans's affection for her and hers for him, though Clint saw from a different perspective and felt sure that Hans had only been using Marie for the convenience of putting his espionage plans into effect. The truth was that Hans's goal was to establish a secret headquarters on this land and Marie provided a front for those plans.

Clint asked her how they had come to find this piece of land, and Marie told of how they had traveled east with the show and left the troupe when it stopped in Omaha. They had taken a room in the Blackstone Hotel. "It's the best hotel in Omaha, you know," she said. Marie had always liked nice things.

"Yes, I know. Expensive place to call 'home.'"

"I never questioned where the money came from, or why there was never a shortage of it," said Marie. "I just assumed Hans's family in Germany must have some wealth. Anyway, one evening we were in the hotel bar and a fellow got to talking to Hans. This was in 1933. He said he was a real estate broker and had done business with farmers in Thurston County. He remarked about Hans being German and said that in the 1920s he had lived in southern California in a largely German city called Anaheim. Said he had plans of returning there after he finished his business in Pender."

"Do you recall this broker's name?"

Marie nodded. "He said his name was Herman Schmidt. Then this funny expression came over Hans's face and he said something that really surprised me. He said to this Herman fellow, 'My wife and I are talking about retiring around here. We want to get some land that's away from everything.' Now, you know he never referred to me as his wife before!"

Clint said, "So what happened?"

"That broker got excited too and said he thought he knew of something that would be perfect. He said he had knowledge of investment land and he would be willing to share that information for a small finder's fee of $400. Hans didn't mind that, so Herman Schmidt went to his car and came back with survey papers showing this big piece of land right where we are—land that opened in a hilly ravine with about 500 acres for sale. The papers showed the exact location, the contact person at the Winnebago reservation, all the details."

"And Hans said yes?"

"Hans took out his wallet and handed the broker four hundred-dollar bills, which the broker looked pretty happy to

111

get. He handed all those survey papers to Hans, and that was the last we saw of him. Next day we rented a car and drove north from Omaha to the Winnebago agency. A guide went with us to find the property, and I never saw Hans more excited than he was that day. He was talking about just where we could put the house and a machine shed, about how we could get some cattle. But it was the ravine that he seemed most interested in. By the afternoon, we were back at the agency. Hans negotiated a price he was happy with, and then he surprised me again. He purchased this land with cash *in my name*. Now why would he do that if he didn't love me like crazy?"

Clint shook his head as if he couldn't imagine another reason. He could see in his imagination how it had gone then: how they had left the vaudeville show, arranged for the buildings to be built, not only the home and the building to house farm machines, but down in the ravine, a larger, barnlike structure wired for electricity with gas-powered generators installed in preparation for a shortwave radio station and the other equipment needed for espionage.

As they continued to talk, two old friends and former lovers, Clint noticed again and again how frail Marie had become. She looked so tired. He wondered if Hans was caring for her as he should be.

Marie set her plate aside and picked up her cup of coffee. She turned to face him a little more directly. "Clint, I heard from Lily that you and Carrie are very happy, and I'm so glad. It's worked out for the best for all of us."

Clint said, "Yes, I guess you're right, Marie. But we'll always have the memories we made. I sure missed you, even though I've had all of this life—and it *is* so wonderful—with Carrie. You know…"

Marie interrupted, "Do you still have the lantern?"

"Yes, I do," said Clint.

"Well, you keep it. It is ours, and it's a remembrance for just the two of us."

Keep love in your heart. A life without it is like a sunless garden when the flowers are dead
— Oscar Wilde

CHAPTER 7
FINAL CONFRONTATIONS

Before Clint and son Frank left, Marie said, "Clint, it's so great to see you. We'll get together now when Hans gets back. We have so much to talk about. You and your boy get on home, and I'll be seeing you soon."

Clint said, "Yes, Marie. And you take care now, and I'll be back in touch with you in a short while."

So, they left. The old Ford seemed to run pretty well, on down to the main road, cutting across to the little town of Thurston and on into home.

It was about seven-thirty that evening that they got home. They walked into the kitchen, and Carrie was waiting for them. She said, "Clint, you're so late. Where have you been?"

Clint was about to tell her when son Frank burst out, "Oh, Mom, this was really something! Our car got too hot and we had to stop. Dad got into the driveway of this house, and this very nice lady—her name was Marie. He was able to get water for the radiator, and then she had us stay and got us some lunch. She got me all of her albums and pictures and things. Dad knew Marie from years ago, he said, and they were having a great time. Dad went out and got some water and filled the radiator and looked around. He came back and we got ready to go home."

Carrie had heard more than enough. She turned toward Clint with a look of outrage. "Clint, what did you do? You stopped to see that woman? How did you know she was there?"

Clint said, "I didn't know anything about it. I haven't seen her in many, many years."

"Clint! That woman! What are you doing?"

Son Frank sat there listening, and Carrie said to him: "You go up and get to bed. You have to go to school in the morning." As soon as Frank had left the room, she said, "Now, Clint, what's going on?"

Clint said, "I just stopped. We had to get the car fixed, and it was a place to stop. I haven't seen Marie in, I'll tell you, it was way back before the war. It's all nothing. It's been over with—my God, Carrie, it's just us. I don't know anything about anything; I didn't even know she was in the area. It sounds like she and this man she used to travel with have bought a little farm over near the Winnebago agency, and I guess that's where they're living. That's all I know. Yeah, we had to talk a little bit about old times, and that was it."

"Well, I'm really unhappy."

It went on that evening, and it was not very quiet. Things seemed to calm down the next day and life went on. Clint just knew that he had not done well by Carrie. He apologized for everything. He didn't know what to do, except that they needed to get past this because now it was getting on, pretty soon, to the fall of the year and they had to get some things done and settled for winter, even though it was still near the end of September.

Clint said, "Well, look, Carrie. Let's go on into town. There's a big celebration in town, and there's going to be a carnival and I guess some kind of a little circus. Now, we've still got a little bit of money left, and I want you to go into town and do some shopping. You need to get some things. Maybe we can have some dinner in town."

Carrie said, "Well, okay. I think that's what we ought to do."

So, that Saturday, they got into the old Model A and got it running. They drove on in, and Carrie left to go shopping, and Clint said, "I'll be around. If you're going to stop at Alnna's place, that's where I'll see you a little later. We'll get some dinner. You enjoy yourself now. I've got to see a couple of guys. I want to see Duncan Laird and some of the other folks, and get something figured out of what we're going to be able to do here now. Maybe we can get some fall planning, I'm not sure."

Clint walked on down across the railroad tracks, thinking about Duncan as he walked, hearing in his mind the lines of verse his old friend loved to spout: *I am a bard of no regard wi' gentlefolks, and a' that*, and *I am a son of Mars, who have been in many wars, and show my cuts and scars wherever I come; this here was for a wench, and that other in a trench when welcoming the French at the sound of the drum…*

On he walked, out to the field where the carnival with the circus and sideshow was set up. It was about six o'clock, and here at the carnival at the corner was the big sideshow, and here the barker was, all ready for the first show. He was talking: "Come on, come on, come on, all! See the famous Lily Lupino and her entourage, just back from onstage in New York and Chicago! You're going to get to see it all, and here she is. Come on out, Lily! Show 'em all!"

Lily came out with her four girls. There was music in the background.

The barker said, "Look, boys! Watch her shake it, break it, hang it on the wall! Boys, this is your chance to see the show!"

Clint walked by and stood there. Then, as he stood watching Lily Lupino on stage, he realized that she had winked at him and gestured to the left. Clint slipped out and went around to the side and back of the tent. Shortly, a woman showed up. She said, "I'm Ida. Lily sent me." Without another word, she handed him a folded piece of paper, winked, and immediately turned to leave.

Clint took the paper, walked away, and then opened the paper up. Printed on it were what appeared to be some dates and times: "11-11-36-8-AM. Highway side road." That was it. As best as he could figure out, this meant that he was to be at the intersection of the road and the highway at eight a.m. the morning of November 11th. He could only believe that this was the time spoken of by the two men with whom he'd had the earlier conversation and meeting.

Now he had to prepare. *How can I tell Carrie? How can I tell her anything?* When the time came, he decided, he would tell her that he had to go into town to meet with the Farm Home Administration man on his application for the grant, and, if he had to, go back over to the reservation to the agency to further check on the leases for the next season. He hated planning to deceive Carrie, but he had made the commitment to help Jim Phillips and Tom Rosenfeldt, and he intended to keep his commitment.

When October came, Clint began keeping an eye on the sky, watching for the return of the whooping cranes. In this time of severe drought, it was more important to him than ever that the cranes come to the refuge he had created for them, a one-acre plot across the road from the bridge and down in the meadow where a pond had formed, fed by the stream. The huge cranes, most of them with a wingspan exceeding six feet, rested a day or two at the pond, and then moved on. They had come to symbolize hope, as they stopped for refuge on their migration from central Canada south. Even though their numbers were decreasing, they still came each year, and that was enough to keep him believing that nature would yet turn things around for his farm.

He had already checked the refuge acre a few days before, but he went again, just to see that the crows had not made a mess of the corn, oats, and grasses that he intended for the cranes.

Clint kept watch, and one day he heard the trumpeting in the sky that signaled the coming of the cranes. His heart lifted, and he kept well back from the acre to make sure the cranes would come to land, rest, and feed. Only seventeen individual cranes arrived, pausing their migration south. From a hillside across the way, Clint watched as each one flew in on its wide wingspan, then closed its wings and stood on its long legs inspecting the refuge. If they knew he stood watch, they gave no sign of discomfort with his presence.

Clint sat with his shotgun, at peace to see the cranes enjoying the acre, at peace with himself. If the coyotes on the opposite peaks began howling to each other, he would fire a shot into the air to remind them to stick to their rabbits and pheasants; the cranes were not for them. The black crows high up in the cottonwoods knew that their turn would come only after the cranes had gone.

This year, after resting and feeding for three days, the cranes became restless, and on the fourth morning, which was unusually balmy, Clint could see clouds forming and rolling in the south sky. It was so warm, he took off his jacket. He watched the cranes, one by one, begin to spread their wings and take flight. When all of them were airborne, they grouped and slowly circled in a loop that encompassed the sky above the refuge acre and above where Clint waited on the hillside, then they gained flight and headed directly south.

For another hour or two he sat overlooking the refuge as the clouds continued to come in, finally bringing the first drops of gentle rain to fall since March. Rain fell all that day, that night, and all the next day and night, and the drought was at last broken. In Clint's mind, it was all of a piece: the cranes, the rain, his recent meeting with Marie. *Could be my life is changing again. Aren't these all harbingers of change?* Now he turned his full attention to the meeting with Hans.

The 11th of November came, and the car didn't run that morning. It was a cold morning. He couldn't get the car started. He went back into the house to put on his warm jacket and winter cap. He said to Carrie, "I'm going to walk to the highway and get a ride. I'll see you just as soon as I can, but I've got to make sure that I can get that grant like these other farmers are getting. I'm going to find out what the problem is. Now, you and Frankie be good. I'll be with you just as quick as I can."

Carrie said, "All right. You be safe, Clint. Do you have any money?"

He said, "Well, I have a couple of dollars in my pocket. I think maybe that will do it. We don't have anything left of the money Mr. Haskell gave us."

Clint left and walked the two miles. It took him about forty-five minutes because it was slow-going, up and down the hill to the highway. As he got up to the edge of the highway, at the intersection, here came—he recognized it—the black Ford. In the Ford were the driver and two men in the backseat. They pulled over and stopped. Clint opened the door and got in the front seat and said, "Good morning."

In the car driving was Jim Phillips, the FBI agent. In the backseat were Tom Rosenfeldt, the Secret Service man, and another Secret Service agent who was introduced as Harry Johnson. "We're on our way, Clint," said Jim. "Do you have the maps with you and the layout?"

Clint said, "Yes. It's in my pocket." He opened up his sketches and notes, and Jim studied them for a few minutes, then handed them to the two Secret Service agents, who would study them during the drive.

Jim said, "Clint, now, this is what we want you to do. We want you to be ready to come in to the main driveway. We're going to let you out, and we're going to have to go clear around to the back and get as close as we can to the lower part of the fenced area near the main building down in the ravine. We know that Hans is there. If you meet him in the house, I hope you can get him down to the main building. If not, certainly you want to see Marie and talk to her. Then, however it works, as you get down to the main building in the ravine, either with Hans or by yourself, just raise your arm and we'll watch. I have the binoculars, and we'll know then that's where you are going."

Once at Marie's house, Clint went on inside to see Marie. She was alone and very ill. She was sitting up in bed. She said, "Oh, Clint. So nice to see you. Hans is here. He's down in his office and I know he would like to see you too. And I think Lily is going to come and visit." She sounded very weak.

Clint talked for a bit. He said, "Yes, I think Lily will be here." Anger hit him then, rage in full force that Hans had not taken care of Marie, had allowed her to become so ill without proper care and medical attention.

Marie said, "Well now, you've not met Lily, have you?"

He stuffed his anger down so that Marie would not see it and feel concern about it. He didn't want her to be worried. He said, "No, but I've heard many good things about Lily, what you've told me. I think it's time for me to talk to Hans—you said he is down in his office? In the building down below in the ravine?"

She said, "Yes." She reached out her hand and held his arm for a moment.

"Well," he said, "I think it's best for me to go down and see Hans. Lily will be here in a moment. I know she's on her way. And we'll all get together."

Marie said, "Oh, this is really going to be nice."

Clint could see that she barely had the strength to hold her head up.

Leaving the house through the kitchen, he saw four coffee cups on saucers on the table. Now he knew that Hans was not alone. Then he saw two vehicles arrive: first a car driven by Lily, and behind it an ambulance. As Lily parked, the ambulance pulled up to the front door. The medics unloaded a stretcher from the ambulance and followed Lily into the house. They soon came back out with Marie on the stretcher and got her into the ambulance. Then the ambulance pulled away with Lily following in her own car, on their way north to Sioux City to the hospital.

Clint raised his arm up high, and Jim could see through the binoculars that he was alone. Clint, not knowing what he was going to find, or if he would be discovered by the Germans before he got to the barn, took his .38 out by his side, and walked on down to the building.

He moved to the side door of the building and opened it quietly. The plan that had been worked out by Jim Phillips and Tom Rosenfeldt called for Clint to engage Hans in conversation, giving Jim a chance to get into position to capture Hans alive— or shoot, if necessary. Things didn't quite go as hoped. The lights were on as Clint stepped inside, and he could see Hans over to the back of the building at his desk inside a nicely furnished office area with a small sofa and a side chair to the right. As Clint came in, Hans looked up. Clint said, "Hans, I'm Clint. I've been up to see Marie, and I've come down to meet you and say hello."

Hans said, "Oh, it's you. Clinton Morgan. Yes, Marie has told me about you, and now we have met. I want to tell you, Clint, it's your time now." Hans turned quickly and from the open left-hand drawer of the desk he grabbed his Luger and brought it up. Clint immediately leaned to the right. He was within six feet of Hans—and he knew that his position was all wrong for Jim's plan to work. He was directly in the FBI agent's line of fire. There would be no capturing Hans alive, and since Hans clearly intended to shoot him, he had no choice but to fend for himself. It was up to him. He brought his .38 up to his side just as Hans fired once. Clint wheeled and got off two quick shots, one hitting Hans in the neck and the second, right through the chest. Hans slumped over his desk. As Clint moved down behind the chair, he looked to the side window of the office as a man in coveralls was walking by. The man came around inside and had his Luger in his hand. He was young, tall, and blond, and wearing coveralls. He walked swiftly toward Hans. Clint waited two seconds in case Jim could get clear sight on the young German. When no shot rang out from the FBI agent, Clint knew that Jim's line of fire was still too risky. Clint aimed carefully. With his .38 in one hand, steadied by his other, he aimed directly at the tall, young man. His first shot hit him through the side of his head; the second one, in the gut. The man slumped and fell down beside the desk.

In less than sixty seconds of silent fury punctuated by the sounds of gunfire, four men lay dead. Hans von Essen lay across his desk and his assistant was on the floor at his feet. At the rear of the barn, two men, hearing the gunfire, came running from the radio transmitter antennas. As they neared the rear door, they fired their Lugers into the open doorway. The two Secret Service agents, one at each corner of the barn, opened up with their Tommy guns. Five quick shot bursts brought the Germans down at the door.

Clint rose from behind the chair and as he turned to the left, Jim Phillips took him by the shoulders. Jim said, "Clint, it's okay. It's over. You're a brave man. We thought we could keep you safe and still get Hans alive. That turned out not to be possible, but it's all right. We think we have found a treasure trove of German intelligence. Clint, now come with me."

They walked back through the building to an open area, and to the right were barn-door openings. To the left sat a brand-new 1936 four-door, deluxe Ford sedan. Jim handed Clint the keys to the car and as he did, Rosenfeldt came up. In his hand was a Tommy gun. Rosenfeldt said, "It's over with. Clint, we have to get you out of here—now! You'll not hear from us again. Thank you for all of your help, and all things will be taken care of. But we want to reemphasize to you, Clint, that you're never to reveal anything about this to anyone. As far as you're concerned, this never happened."

Once again, Jim said, "Clint, you are a brave man, and your help and service won't be forgotten. You will be well compensated now and in a few months. What we want you to do is back out with the car and drive directly to the county seat in Pender to the Farm Home Administration office. There you'll see Mr. Griffith. You will be taken care of there and on your way. Now, be off with you. And, Clint," Jim said. "Here. I know you're a little short of cash. In fact, you probably don't have any, do you?"

Clint said, "Well, not much."

"Here's fifty dollars, expense money. That should take care of you for the rest of the day and as things go along. We have much to do. Good luck. Goodbye. Thank you so much."

Clint, stoic, shook hands with Jim and the other agents. "Jim, Tom, that which we have experienced together will be with me always. I shall miss you both." He got into the car and saw that the gas tank was half full. He started the engine and they helped him back out. He drove up the lane. Just before he got to the road that would take him to the main highway, he pulled the car to the side and stopped. He sat for a moment, breathing deeply and letting the facts roll through his mind. He had killed again. He raised his hand to his forehead. *Two men this time.* He closed his eyes, seeing them again, one by one: the young German, Hans, Frenchie, Fredrik. Then he let his head rest more heavily in his hand as he thought about Marie, on her way in the ambulance. *Oh, Marie.*

For some moments, he sat with his grief. Finally, he sat up straight, looked around in all directions, then drove the car back onto the road and across over to the main highway that would take him into Pender and to the Farm Home Administration.

In about thirty minutes he was there. It was still not yet noon. He walked in. Mr. Griffith was at his desk. He looked up and said, "Clint, I have good news for you. Your loan has been approved. Come on in and sit down."

Clint sat down.

Mr. Griffith said, "Clint, I think you need a cup of coffee."

Clint said, "I sure do."

He poured a nice, hot cup of coffee. Clint took a long sip and then another drink.

Mr. Griffith said, "Let's get this taken care of. Now, there are going to be some things that you have to do here. I've got some papers we have to sign and things we have to take care of. Now, don't be too concerned about it. I must tell you: this grant is quite substantial. It's more than the usual. It's $2800."

Clint looked at him in amazement and said, "What did you say?"

"Twenty-eight hundred, Clint. It's yours. Now, however, we have to fill out papers and as we expend these funds, we have to have a record of it. But don't worry about it; I'll help you with it; we'll take care of it. Right now, I want you to sign these, and as you sign them, I'm going to get this checkbook ready. The $2800 has been deposited for you. We need to have this remain in some confidence. It is in a national bank in Omaha. The check blanks are made out to your account, and as you expend the money and sign each one, you must have a receipt. Of course, the money is to help you get started again, and we'll take care of everything. Here's your checkbook. You come back now, let's say—this is the 11th—let's try to get back together next Monday. Meanwhile, I know you've got a lot to do."

Clint got up. They shook hands. In utter amazement, Clint walked out to the car, thought for a moment, then drove out of town north on the highway to Emerson. He stopped in Emerson, put gas in the car, and went on to Dakota City. He hadn't had anything to eat. There he stopped at a little restaurant and had another cup of coffee and a sandwich, then on to Sioux City, to the hospital.

In the hospital, he inquired about the room of Marie Mahoney and where Lily Lupino was. Then he went on up to the third floor, into the room, and there he found Marie in the hospital bed and Lily beside her. He walked over to Marie.

Marie opened her eyes and spoke: "Oh, Clint, it's so good to see you again. And Lily is here with me." But her voice was so weak. It was obvious that she had been given morphine or some other pain medication. But she recognized Clint. He sat beside her and held her hand. Marie looked at him and said, "It is something. Don't you remember so much, Clint? The thing I remember most is you rescuing me from that terrible place and the lantern. And we have the lantern. And you remember that night and the lantern." With that, Marie's voice faded away. Clint held her hand, gently kissed her and held her for a moment. She was sleeping but her breath was labored.

He stood up then and said to Lily, "I am going to step out for a little while, but I'll be back." He didn't mention it aloud, not wanting to risk having Marie overhear him, but he was going to the mortuary to make the final arrangements.

Lily walked with him to the door, where she said quietly, "She really does not have much more time."

"I know. I'll be back," he repeated.

So, Clint left the hospital. It was only a few blocks away to the mortuary. It was now late afternoon. He went into the mortuary and made the arrangements for Marie's cremation and for her ashes to be held for him until a time when he would come to get them. He wrote a check for all of the services. He left instructions for the mortuary to await contact from Lily Lupino with the directions and time to pick up and transport Marie's remains.

As he reentered Marie's hospital room, he knew instantly that she would be gone very soon. Lily knew it too and stood on the far side of Marie's bed, holding her hand. He took his place and caught up her other hand. He could tell that she was unconscious now. *She's only forty-one.* The thought of how young she was kept recurring to him, troubling him. The ravages of the cancer had not only marred her beauty but had stolen her future as well. Even so, he could not stop looking at her. And so it was that the two people in the world who had loved Marie the most were beside her, holding her hands, as she passed away.

They each kissed her one last time as the hospital personnel entered the room and gently encouraged them to leave. At first they said nothing to each other, walking down the long corridor, side by side, but then they took refuge in the necessary details. Clint told Lily the name of the mortuary that would await word from her and discussed the arrangements he had made. When it was her turn, she spoke with a surprisingly clear voice: "Don't worry about the car. I'll take care of the transfer of title. Everything is in Marie's name, you know. Nothing was in Hans's name."

He and Lily parted on the front steps of the hospital. Reaching his car, Clint drove out of town, past the stockyards to the Stockyard Hotel. He registered and went up to his room. There, in total exhaustion, he sat down in wonder of a day that he could never have imagined would have happened. His grief for Marie overtook him then, and he made no effort to suppress it. Marie deserved that much. His heart ached with the realization that he would never see her again.

The next morning he checked out of the hotel, drove over to the Stockyard Restaurant, had some breakfast, and then went down to the yards. He found the stockyards commission man, John Moore, whom he knew, a man whom he trusted. He made a time to meet with him as the sales of the morning were drawing to a close.

Clint waited and when John Moore came, they sat down. Clint said, "I'm going to ask you to represent me. I need to have a purchase of farm animals and horses. I want some cows coming fresh, brood sows. I've just gotten a Farm Home Administration grant. I need to equip and refurnish everything at the farm with my animals. I need hay and grain. My estimation is that this is going to be an expenditure of around a thousand dollars or thereabouts. Now, I can tell you a little bit. I know that I need two teams of horses; I need four milk cows coming fresh; I need six brood sows; I need hay, grain; I probably need some new harness and wagon; then if you can think of anything else essential to that.

"I would want you to secure the best that you can. I want them delivered no later than December 10th. I will be willing to give you some up-front cash of about $500. I have to have receipts for each thing. I trust you, as we have done business in the past in selling my hogs and the like. If you have any questions, you're going to have to get in touch with me directly at the farm, but we then will settle up. You can look for twenty percent or more commission for your services, plus any expenses you may have incurred, delivery and the like. Do we have a deal?"

John Moore looked at Clint and said, "You'll be taken care of, and I'll get you the best I can."

Clint said, "That's good. I'll be seeing you."

Clint left and went back to his car. It was near noon. He drove back across the Missouri River and stopped in South Sioux City at his favorite store, John's Meat Market and Grocery Store, and there he did some shopping. He knew the things that Carrie needed and that they needed at home. He got fresh bacon, a ham, a beef roast, and then some other items that would tide them over: fifty-pound sack of flour, fifty-pound sack of sugar, some other things. He didn't have much room left, but he added a couple of big chunks of coal that he could break up for the kitchen stove. He also got oranges and other fresh fruits and vegetables: cabbages, carrots, and things that the grocer picked out for him.

He loaded them up. The back seat was completely full, and he was on his way home from there.

It was late in the afternoon. There in the kitchen was Carrie waiting, wondering and worried. Clint came in with a smile, grabbed her with a big embrace, and said, "Carrie, this is it. We have the grant; I have the cash; I got things for us that are in the car. We need to unload them. I'll be talking to you about everything, but we're going to be okay for the next year. We're going to get all of the new livestock, new milk cows; we're going to have enough money so you can get the chickens that we need to raise—and everything else. It's going to be great. You'll be able to get some shoes and clothing for son Frank and things for yourself. We're going to talk about it. Let's get everything unloaded.

"And I'm kind of hungry, and I'll bet you are too. Let's see what we can have here for dinner. Maybe some of the fresh pork chops I got, or I've got a nice beef roast. You know, it's the time—we used to get them at Christmastime—I do have a quart container of fresh oysters. And I stopped at a dairy and got a couple of gallons of milk and cream, so let's have some oyster stew. And I didn't know where we were on coffee, but I got a couple of cans of coffee, so we're going to have enough of that. We're in pretty good shape, Carrie."

So, they had a wonderful celebration that evening. The rest of the year, and the years beyond, looked very bright and promising.

Meanwhile, at the farm established by Hans and owned by Marie, the agents found all, and more, that they were looking for. Under the garage area was what appeared to be a huge concrete vault with a steel door, and inside, to the side, was a high-voltage, natural-gas-powered generator. In the room were shortwave radio transmitters, receivers, a table with maps, and an Enigma—the secret German coding machine. Radio frequency codes were ready for communication of landing sites to agents waiting aboard U-boats, the German submarines patrolling off the Atlantic and Gulf coasts of the United States. Lined up on a wall was a small armament of rifles, Lugers, submachine guns, hand grenades, and a few other things. It was a wonderful trove of all of the information that Hans had accumulated to go out as new agents came into the country.

They had captured all of it. Their effort now was to destroy all evidence. After the agents finished cleaning up everything, the bodies of Hans and his three men were buried deep inside the concrete vault, stripped of all identification, and covered, as was all of the rest of the evidence of the vault and the barn. The antennas that were in place on the hillside were all taken out and destroyed, with no evidence remaining.

Lily took charge of the farm, staying on in the house for a year to settle the estate and allow the land to lie fallow, become overgrown, and return to its natural state. She gathered all mail that arrived at the farm and made regular deliveries of mail to a Secret Service courier stationed at the Winnebago Indian agency.

Meanwhile, Clint went on into the year 1937. He was able to bring back the life of his farm, and the year and crops were very, very good. Early that fall, the same original black Ford made another stop at Clint's farm. As it came into the driveway, Clint went up to the car. The passenger door opened, and Mr. Haskell stepped out.

Mr. Haskell greeted Clint and said, "Looks like you got a good year, Clint. Things are looking very well."

Clint said, "Yes, it is all much better."

Mr. Haskell said, "Had you heard that Wyoming's state senator and former governor Robert Carey died earlier this year? I know that you and Bob were close friends."

Clint felt the shock go through him. "Awfully young, wasn't he? What happened?"

"Yes, only fifty-eight. Heart failure."

Clint bowed his head at the news, but Mr. Haskell moved to the business at hand and gestured toward the car. "Now, you've met my businessman, and Jim here with me. Now, Clint, I want to talk to you about a couple of things. I have something for you, and if you don't mind, we'll just step away a little bit, and I'm going to give this to you. What it is, is the deed to the farm—everything, free and clear. Now, Clint, this has been arranged for me to give to you. It is from anonymous sources, but those who are grateful for your service and your friendship of past years. Now, the only thing about it is, you will have to pay the taxes for the year. It's yours, Clint. Let's keep in touch. Continued good luck and we'll see you again."

They shook hands. Clint stood, stunned, not quite able to relate to what was happening to him. Mr. Haskell got back into the car, which then drove away. There he stood with the deed in his hands. Then he turned and walked down to the house to Carrie.

He walked into the kitchen and Carrie said, "Who was that? Was that Mr. Haskell again?"

Clint said, "Yes. Carrie, you aren't going to believe this, but I have the deed to the farm. He gave it to me. It is free and clear, and it is ours."

Carrie said, "Oh my! What ... how?"

Clint said, "I don't know, except that it's from Mr. Haskell and others thanking me for my loyalty and friendship from years past, and it's ours."

That evening Clint sat looking at the deed. The farm was truly his now. He calculated that at current farmland values, it had to be worth at least $35,000. Counting that and the grant, car, and cash, he had been paid more than $40,000. No small sum in 1937.

Fresh in his mind was the showdown with the bank president at a neighbor's farm just two days earlier. Clint had learned from a director of the bank that the president intended to foreclose on a farm just two miles north. The widow Hunter was trying to survive, keep the farm and raise two young daughters. Because of the terrible year of 1936, she had been unable to make her payments. Now in 1937, she was hoping that the first harvest of grains would bring enough to make a payment on the note, but the bank president wasn't planning to wait long enough to find out. He and his attorney were going to drive out to the Hunter farm, present her with a foreclosure notice, and force her to leave immediately. When Clint learned about this, he informed five of the other neighbors.

The morning that the banker drove up to Mrs. Hunter's gate, he found five men there with Clint, all with shotguns. The banker and his attorney were in the first car to come down the hill to the gate. In the second car was the sheriff with two deputies. After seeing the armed farmers at the gate, the bank president started to get out of his car, but the sheriff came up and spoke to him, loud enough for Clint and the other farmers to hear. The sheriff said, "In all good conscience, I can't be here to protect you. I must be here to protect Mrs. Hunter and these good men who have confronted you and intend not to allow you to go any further. Now, you get back into your car with your attorney and leave." The banker, visibly shaken, did just that. His car turned around and drove back up the hill. No further word was spoken. Clint and his five neighbors turned and went home. Mrs. Hunter was ever grateful for the kindness shown and the help her neighbors gave her.

In the subsequent months, Mrs. Hunter was able to make a small payment on her loan and also saw the loan renegotiated. She managed to survive and keep the farm. The banker never again attempted to take a farmer's home and land by foreclosure in that manner.

Considering now his net worth, Clint realized that he no longer needed the bank president nor had to hear his cutting remarks in refusal of a loan. Clint's net worth gave him a working cash flow at any local bank he chose.

A few months into 1938, word came to Clint that Mr. Griffith wanted to see him. An appointment time was set, and Clint went to the Farm Home Administration office. After shaking hands, Mr. Griffith said, "Clint, go on to the back room. There's a guest waiting to see you there."

Lily Lupino sat waiting at a table. She had a cup of coffee in her hands and another steaming cup had been poured for Clint. She smiled. "How's that car working out for you, Clint?"

He pulled back the chair to take a seat. "It's doing fine, Lily. How are you?"

Almost immediately Lily got down to business. "Everything with the funeral home went exactly as you instructed," she said. After Marie's passing, Lily had contacted the mortuary to put into effect Clint's order for cremation, with the ashes to be held until such time as Clint would come to collect them. "Then I returned to Marie's farm and began the inventory of her furnishings and personal belongings. You know that in her will, Marie left the house, the farm, and all of the machinery to me."

Clint nodded again. He picked up his cup and drank half of the hot coffee down.

"Well, what you don't know," Lily went on, "is that when the Secret Service went through that office where Hans died…" she paused and looked at Clint until he looked up and met her eyes, "…they found a duplicate copy of Marie's will where Hans had altered the beneficiary."

Now Lily focused on her own cup of coffee while Clint simmered with that news. Finally Clint asked, "So whose name was Hans changing it to?"

"Clint, I think you knew that Hans had a wife and family in Germany, right?"

"Yes."

"Apparently the wife's name was Criselda. The name he had written in was Criselda von Essen. He was trying to put the farm in his German wife's name."

With sorrow in his heart, Clint remembered Marie recounting the story of how Hans had acquired the lease

133

information from Herman Schmidt, how he had told Herman that the farm was for his and his wife's retirement.

Clint said, "Do you think Marie ever knew?"

"No, I am quite sure she didn't, and I am forever grateful for that. It would have hurt her deeply." Lily kept her eyes on her coffee cup until the urge to tears subsided. "I saw her only occasionally after they got that farm where Hans was setting up for his mission. But I could tell in the last years that her illness was coming on. It really started when they were still performing but she never let on. I'm not sure she actually realized that her health was failing or that her performances were beginning to suffer."

Lily stopped to clear her throat. When she spoke again, she changed the subject. "So they each offered the other something, didn't they. Hans needed her as a front for his espionage ring, and she needed him for the easier life he could afford to give her."

Lily stayed in Pender as long as it took to settle Marie's estate. In her own surreptitious way, she moved about the community, still a Secret Service agent, searching for any other German agents who might have located in the area. After the land had lain fallow for a year, she leased it out in 1938 and sold all of the farm equipment to the man who leased the land. Before she left Pender, she participated in a geek show to help out her carnival friends in the area who were down on their luck.

Then, when she was satisfied that she had done her job, both for Marie and for the Secret Service, she returned to San Francisco and with the income from the farm, she lived a comfortable life in the gay and entertainment district. Eventually, she saw her responsibilities for the Secret Service begin more and more to focus on the Japanese. As life went on, she later sold the farm and with those proceeds, she spent the rest of her life in San Francisco.

Clint and Carrie continued on their farm. By 1939, Frank was a teenager in high school, and both of the older children were out of the house and on their own. Ardell had apprenticed with a certified public accountant until he had learned enough to take the certification test, which he had passed on the first try and now had his own CPA business. Clarabelle had given up teaching to move to San Francisco, where she had taken a management position with the Mark Hopkins Hotel.

Son Frank, in Clint's eyes, was a different story from the two stepchildren. Perhaps he had put so much effort into building a relationship with Ardell, as much to please Carrie as anything else, there was just not much left to put into building a relationship with Frank. While Carrie had always maintained strong relationships with all three of her children, valuing them for the individuals they were, Clint was always more focused on what they *did*.

It wasn't that Clint never tried. About 1940, when Frank was in the tenth grade, he spotted a pair of black boots in the window of Mr. Murray's menswear store in town. They were priced at $9.95, and Frank thought they were a thing of beauty. He really wanted them, and he convinced Clint to go with him to look at the boots. He knew that Mr. Murray, who was also a director at the bank, was a friend of Clint's. Once inside the store, Frank breathed in deeply of the smell of new clothes and fine leather. He was measured, and Mr. Murray went to the back to see if he had the boots in the right size: 8-1/2. In the box he brought out were the boots. Frank tried them on and they fit perfectly.

Clint could see that there would be no separating the boy from those boots. "What do you think?" he asked.

Mr. Murray spoke up: "He needs a couple of pairs of boot socks."

Clint nodded agreement. "He's got to have something to keep dry."

Mr. Murray added a bottle of 100% pure Neatsfoot Oil to the pile on the counter, to preserve and waterproof the boots. Mr. Murray rang up the items, which came to $15.00. Frank walked out wearing the boots.

What bonding between Clint and his son occurred with the new boots was soon diminished when Frank asked for a dollar to go with his class to Lincoln.

"What's it for?" Clint asked.

"It's for a journalism conference," said Frank.

"You don't need that!"

Neither Clint nor Frank could have put into words the conflict that stood between them. Though he would never have said so, Clint wanted his son to emulate him, to be the same successful horseman/cowboy/farmer that he was, but Frank's interests were entirely elsewhere. At the same time, Clint had always admired his own younger brother who had left the Nebraska farmlands to pursue education, eventually becoming a professor. Clint's interests in education, reading, philosophy, and politics had always been important to him, something to engage in on the side, but he could never have made them his life's work. He could not accept that Frank might make the choices for his life that he himself had not been able to make.

Immediately after high school, Frank enlisted in the Army Air Corps. This was at the beginning of the war years. He served well in the service, and came home in late 1945, back home to see his mother and father.

Carrie was so happy, greeting her son. Clint appeared pleased but did not seem as happy with his son as might be expected. The house was quieter than Frank had remembered it. Clarabelle was by then in her early thirties, living as a single woman making her own way in California, and Ardell was in

136

Oregon. Questions revolved in Frank's mind about Clint's feeling towards him. Things had never been the same between them after that very first meeting of Frank with Marie. Why? Now home from military service, meeting with friends in town, and planning to spend a few days with his parents, Frank knew that Clint was very troubled by his presence. He knew that he could not stay.

On the morning of January 3, 1946, Clint was out in the corrals and the barns, and Frank came out looking for him. He thought he would talk to his father a little bit about how things were. Clint looked up and said, "Tell me: what are you going to do?"

His son said, "Well, I'm going to go to university. I don't know what I will do then. I may be an attorney, maybe I'll work for a newspaper and get a writing career. I might even go south to get into acting and entertainment. But I can't stay here."

Clint looked at him and said, "Good, because I don't want you. I don't want you here, I don't want you about. I want you to leave, and I want you to leave now. I want you to go in, pack your things, say goodbye to your mother. Meanwhile, I'll hitch up the team of horses to the wagon."

Frank looked at him and said not a word. He went in, said goodbye to his mother, and got his flight bag. His mother was in tears. He had nothing to say except goodbye. The reason they took the wagon instead of the Ford is that the Ford—that same, old 1936 Ford—sat there with its block cracked and frozen. Clint hadn't taken care of it.

They got into the wagon, and Clint took his son the two miles from home to the highway. There at the highway, Frank took his bag and got out of the wagon. Clint turned the wagon around. They said nothing to each other. As Frank got to the edge of the road, a car came by and stopped. The driver said, "Where you going, soldier?"

"I'm going to where the bus is in West Point, then I'm going on to Omaha."

The driver said, "Good, because my daughter's here. We're going to the bus. She has to go back to Lincoln to start her winter term at University of Nebraska. Get in, son."

That was the last that Frank saw of his father.

Clint and Carrie went on through 1946 to the next year. Clint sold the farm. He sold all of their farm equipment and bought a nice home in town, and there they spent their retirement years. But it was not a happy retirement. Carrie was not happy to leave the farm, nor was she happy to see her husband withdraw more and more. It was just the two of them now, with the three children gone. Though he and Carrie traveled some, nothing lifted Clint's spirits.

They never mentioned their son Frank between them again. However, after they had left the farm, Carrie regularly sent birthday and Christmas cards to Frank, and in 1947 she visited him along with Ardell on a trip she took alone to Oregon. Frank was at the university by that time. Upon her return to Pender, she told her husband about Ardell but nothing about Frank.

If Clint thought that the worst events of his life were in his past, he was wrong. In 1954, Carrie finally agreed to see a doctor to ask about the pains and fatigue that had been increasing over the previous six months. It was inconceivable to Clint that anything could be seriously amiss with Carrie. She had always been so healthy and so strong. He did not know that it was more a matter that she was not inclined to speak about signs of ill health. But when the doctor diagnosed Stage 4 cancer, neither of them could continue to deny what lay ahead for them. It was as though having to state her diagnosis aloud removed the last support Carrie was leaning on, and from that point, her health deteriorated rapidly. She was hospitalized for intensive treatment, then soon moved to a nursing home where she passed away in 1955.

For three months, Clint moved about their home with little sleep and an even worse record for decent food. He mostly sat on the sofa and stared into the room, not seeing anything but memories.

Then one day his memories of Carrie were balanced with his returning memories of Marie, and with his thoughts of Marie came his terrible memories of the killings, all of them related in one way or another to Marie. He had killed four men, and the memories began again to weigh on his mind. He could see their faces at the moment he shot them; he could see them going down, dying in front of him. The images never left him; if anything, they became more vivid as time passed. He never talked about any of it but he could not overcome the depression, and the strain of it showed in his face. Just for something to do, he worked for a while as a bartender at the American Legion Club, and he even enjoyed playing poker and gambling there, but always the memories hung over him.

One day toward the end of 1955, Clint remembered Marie's ashes and his pledge to one day collect them from the Sioux City mortuary. A plan took shape in his mind of what he must do and how to go about it. As his plan grew, it included a last trip back to Careyhurst, which had been sold in 1940 to the Kansas City Life Insurance Company, and maybe even a visit with his old friend Frank McDuffie.

He knew that if Carrie were still alive, she would have wanted to go along—she had always loved a trip—and he would have had to tell her that he wanted to go by himself.

He didn't pack much: a change of clothes, his shaving kit, and the duffel bag that held the lantern. These he tossed into the back seat of the car and headed north out of Pender toward Sioux

City. At the mortuary he claimed Marie's ashes and placed them reverently inside the lantern, which he returned to the duffel bag. Then he went directly to the Sioux City airport, where he parked his car and booked a round trip to Cheyenne, Wyoming. In Cheyenne, he rented a car and drove to Douglas, where he went first to the lumberyard and asked that a simple, tongue-and-groove pine box be made for him. A carpenter there proceeded at once to make the box and was finished an hour later. Clint shook his hand and paid him twenty dollars, then loaded the pine box into the back of the rented car and drove to the large ranch he had known as Careyhurst.

The ranch had been renamed Bixby Ranch. Clint introduced himself to the ranch manager, a young man named John Martinez, and explained that he'd been the equine manager there forty years earlier. He described his purpose and asked for permission to travel across the property in order to bury the pine box on the government range land overlooking the Platte Valley.

"I don't see any reason you can't do that," said Martinez. "Let me grab a pickaxe and a couple of shovels, and I'll help you."

"I'd be much obliged," said Clint.

They got along well as they worked together, speaking casually about the changes at the ranch in the decades since Clint had left. When they were finished and Clint placed the last of the rocks for the cairn they had built over the gravesite, Martinez walked off several paces to give Clint a few minutes of privacy. Then, coming down from the ridge, he offered Clint a bed for the night in the workmen's quarters.

"Thanks, John," Clint said. "I'd really appreciate that."

Next morning, Clint thanked the ranch manager again, then drove out to Frank McDuffie's ranch—where he found Frank out at a corral watching his men prepare to move cattle. Frank's look of irritation broke into a grin when he realized that the stranger was Clint, come to visit after so many years. "Did you come to help me herd cattle?" he called as he walked up to Clint's car.

They shook hands and slapped each other on the shoulder. "No, I came to see if you were still keeping out of trouble," said Clint. Then his face lost its smile. Without much in the way of a preamble, he said, "You remember Marie Mahoney, don't you?"

Surprise was evident on Frank's face. "Why yes, why sure I do. I just haven't thought about her in years. Haven't heard the name Mahoney since she left back—what was it, Clint?— 1918, wasn't it?"

"1918, that's right. So long ago."

"What happened to her? I didn't know you'd got back with her."

In a rush of weariness, Clint knew he couldn't tell the story. He tried for a short version: "No, no … we … we never got back together. But I saw her before she died. Marie passed away in 1936. She was only forty-one years old."

Frank looked confused. "I thought I heard somewhere that you married a woman named Carrie, is that right?"

"Yes, I did." He took a deep breath. "My wife died early this year."

"I'm real sorry to hear that, Clint."

Clint nodded. He hurried then to change the subject. "How's your wife, Frank?"

"Oh, Meg's doing good. Always been my best partner."

"And last I saw you, you had two little children. They must be all grown up now."

Frank nodded. "They are. My son has a couple of children of his own. My … my daughter is married to the vice president of the bank in Glenrock. In fact, you should meet her, Clint." He paused. "I mean it. You really should meet her."

He was staring so hard that Clint finally said, "Well, sure. Of course, I remember her as just a little thing. I think she wasn't even two years old when I saw her. Pretty little thing. What was her name?"

"Her name is Marie, Clint. She's named after her mother."

Clint was staring back now.

"Marie Mahoney was her mother." Frank said it quietly.

Something in Clint's head had started to buzz, and he blinked his eyes to try to hear more clearly.

Frank was talking faster now: "You remember that she came here to stay with me and Meg for a short time after you'd been in France a while. But really she stayed just long enough to have the baby, then she left the baby with us to raise."

The facts he was hearing didn't make sense to Clint. "Marie had a baby in 1918 while I was in France? Then it must have been … it couldn't have … are you saying the baby was my child? *My* baby?" The emotions crowding his heart were making his face feel tight.

Frank couldn't have looked more sober if he was describing the death of his mother. "Yes, Clint. The baby was yours, but Marie swore us to secrecy. She begged us to adopt little Marie and raise her as ours. And that's what we did. We were afraid of what might happen to her if we didn't." He took off his Stetson and slapped it against his thigh. "Hell, I hated like everything keeping a thing like that from you. I knew you deserved to know, but Marie asked us to promise we'd never tell. Our Marie herself doesn't know. But of course, Marie Mahoney never did come back for her child, and after a couple of years, we gave up looking for her. You said she passed away in 1936, so I'm not keeping that secret any longer."

Then a sort of urgency came over Frank. "Clint, you need to meet your daughter. Let's go into the house. Meg will be real glad to see you after all these years. What I think we should do is, Meg will go with me to Glenrock and you follow in your car. You can wait at the Higgins for us. Meg and I will talk with Marie and her husband, and we'll all meet you later for dinner at the Paisley Shawl. I'll come find you in the bar. That way we can tell her that you're her father before she meets you face-to-face. How 'bout it? What do you say?"

There was nothing Clint could say. He felt completely mute as he followed Frank into their house and heard him call out to his wife. The woman who came into the room had changed little from the woman he had met so many years earlier. She couldn't have been friendlier or more gracious toward Clint. Soon they were getting into the two cars, and on their way to Glenrock.

Clint parked his rental car on the street right in front of the Higgins Hotel. For a few minutes he sat in the car, just looking at the building, with its bright white siding and green awning over the steps up to the door. Finally he grabbed his jacket and stepped out of the car to go inside. The lobby of the historic hotel was much the same. Even the scent of the air held memories for him. He walked to the Paisley Shawl Restaurant and stood in the doorway, looking in. Strong afternoon sun streamed through the familiar large windows and the gold sconces were lit between the windows. Just as before, dark-wood chairs were drawn up to tables covered with crisp white tablecloths. Wait staff moved about the room and a few diners were beginning to arrive. He walked on to the Antelope Bar, past the piano, and up to the bar.

"What'll you have?" asked the bartender.

"Whiskey. Neat," said Clint.

As he drank the shot, he couldn't hold back the flood of memories. *Here I am back at the Higgins, thirty-eight years after that memorable night Marie and I spent here together. That night we conceived the young woman I'm about to meet as my daughter.* He stared at the row of whiskey bottles arranged neatly on the shelf against the wall behind the bar, then down at the empty shot glass in his hand. *Here is where it all happened, and I'm going to meet my daughter!*

Clint had been in the bar a little more than a half hour when Frank entered, looked at Clint sitting at the bar, and motioned for him to follow. The two walked together into the Paisley Shawl and Clint immediately saw the table where Meg and a young couple waited. The young woman was looking eagerly in his direction.

It would have hurt him less if she had looked more like his own family, and less like her mother. Something around her mouth and something about her eyes struck his heart as soon as he saw Marie. And in an instant, Clint understood at last the difference between his love for Marie and his love for Carrie. His wife had held his affection all those years because she evoked in him feelings of warmth and caring that he had found nowhere else in the world. Marie, on the opposite hand, had always represented mystery and an enticing quality of forever staying just out of his grasp. Carrie had been the warm nest available to him at all times; Marie was the distant vision that would never be his, no matter how many promises were made and how alluring the prize appeared. The young woman now standing before him with her mother's eyes and mouth had that same quality, and Clint couldn't stop himself from glancing at Marie's husband to see if he, too, was haunted. But no, he could see that William Kincaid was not tormented. He was clearly assured of his young wife's devotion. *So she has my spirit, then*, Clint thought. *She looks like her mother, but in her heart she's like me.*

They had dinner together: Frank and Meg McDuffie, Marie and William, and Clint. She was born to be among people, but not performing, like her mother—instead, she was gifted at making the people around her comfortable with each other. William, too, was surprisingly friendly. Both of them appeared to take the news calmly that Frank and Meg had adopted Marie as a baby and that this stranger she had just met for the first time was her father. She met his eyes and looked at him for several seconds, but there was nothing in her gaze that suggested anything but acceptance, with a little curiosity. Even so, William had moved closer to her and put an arm around her in case she needed his protection. Clint was glad to see that, to know that his daughter had found a good man to protect her. *I guess this fellow is my son-in-law. Think of that!*

Toward the end of the long meal together, the young couple began to speak of a car trip they were planning from Glenrock to visit the Oregon coast and north into Western Canada, and Clint realized that it was time to draw the evening to a close. He mentioned that he planned to get a room and stay the night at the hotel, and Marie asked if she could meet him for breakfast the next morning. Clint's heart seemed to rise a little higher.

Breakfast was just the two of them. Marie had a lot of questions and he answered them all, taking advantage of the opportunity to study the face that had already become dear to him. He saw her gaze return again and again to the two-inch scar on his left cheek, so he told her the story of the knife wound he suffered during an annual Horse and Mule Trading Trek West so many years ago. They talked about keeping in touch with each other.

Later, as they were saying their good-byes, he was startled by how easily she moved toward him and hugged him, drawing back then, arms still around him, to look him in the eye when he said, "I'll see you again." Something in her expression, a friendly, forgiving softness around her eyes, made him ache with a sudden awareness of lost years that could never be made up.

Clint did a lot of thinking as he retraced his steps: back to Cheyenne where he returned the rental car and boarded the return flight to Sioux City. There he got into his own car and drove—rather slowly—the miles back to Pender.

There was so much to think about, so many moments of the previous evening and the morning's breakfast kept replaying in his mind. His daughter had claimed her territory in his memory. *How strange life can be. I have been focused for so long on the four lives I took from the world, and here all along there was a life that I brought into the world and didn't even know it.* The thought of it made his heart feel light. He wished for just a moment that he had a picture of her to put in a frame and hang up in his house, but then he realized that nothing would take from him the picture of her that now stood so large in his heart. Over and over he played in his mind a sort of movie of his daughter's face as she spoke, her eyes as she watched him, her clearly joyful devotion to her husband. She was such a bright light. Then it occurred to him that he had another child with whom there were also so many lost years. *I need to write a letter to my son Frank. I need to let him know he has a sister.*

The warm memories of the meeting with his daughter carried him all the way to his front door. But as he stepped inside, it hit him hard that Carrie was not there to greet him. How he longed to hear her call out, "Clint! I'm so glad you're back! Tell me all about your trip—and wait till I tell you what's been going on here."

With Carrie gone, home meant being alone. Some days the loneliness drove him out the door, into his car, just to drive the countryside, out past the old farm, even up to the Winnebago agency and past Marie's farm. Duncan Laird was an old man now, bent over with age, but he still had a ready smile on his face and a few lines of Scottish poetry on his tongue. Duncan rarely made it to town anymore, but Clint visited him at his home. The two continued their friendship until Duncan passed away in 1962.

Clint stopped by to visit Mrs. Hunter, who had managed to keep her farm, though now she hired hands to do most of the field work, while she took care of the chickens and her large garden. They had a nice chat and he enjoyed the fresh pie and coffee she offered. But on the second stop at her house, he realized that she was getting the wrong impression of his intentions, so he didn't go back again.

Just as he had promised, Clint stayed in touch with his daughter, writing regularly and speaking on occasion by telephone. The more they talked about Marie's mother and her dance career with Lily Lupino, the more she spoke about wanting to meet Lily someday. Gradually some trip plans formed. They arranged to meet in Denver, just the two of them, and fly to San Francisco, where Lily greeted them in a style of which few hostesses would be capable. She reserved a room in the Hotel St. Francis for Clint and put Marie up in her own home. Lily clearly enjoyed showing them around San Francisco, but Clint spent most of his time watching Lily's expressions as she took in the remarkable resemblances between this young woman and her longtime friend and loved one. Over dinner in Chinatown, Lily told stories about her friend Marie that he had never heard before, and the three of them laughed despite the heartache.

They visited Golden Gate Park and returned a few times to Polk Street, the Castro, the Tenderloin, and other areas where Lily's friends in the gay and entertainment world lived and worked. At Castro Theatre, they took in a show featuring female impersonators and went backstage with Lily. Again and again a look of amazement came on the faces of aging dancers, Lily and

Marie's friends, as they saw his daughter for the first time and rushed to embrace her. Marie maintained her poise and a smile on her face throughout.

When it was time to end the San Francisco trip, after long hugs all around, Marie made her way directly back to Glenrock, and Clint returned to Nebraska. But he returned with a fresh enthusiasm for his own life. He became a regular patron at the library and began to pursue more seriously his lifetime interests in reading history and philosophy, and now he added travel. He would read up on a particular destination, then book a flight or load up his car and go take a look for himself. Having been financially successful in his farming/ranching life, he still had plenty of money to follow where his interests led him. Because one of his interests had always been horses, he began to read up on the Kentucky Derby. In late April 1958 he packed his car again and drove to Kentucky, ending up at Churchill Downs for the May 3 race. His research told him to place a bet on Lincoln Road to win, but the horse came in second to Tim Tam. After the race, he went down to the paddock to look up a horse trader he had known in the old days in Cheyenne.

Back home in Pender, he asked for more time behind the bar at the American Legion Club serving as a bartender. And when he wasn't serving, he often just hung around, passing the time of day with whoever happened by. He never passed up a poker game or a chance to do a little harmless gambling.

In 1961, Clint's health showed signs of failing, so he moved to Omaha to be near the VA hospital. What ailed him was what ailed many an old cowboy, prostate cancer—the "Cowboy's Lament." Still, he never regretted his many years in the saddle. He overcame the cancer then, but he was no longer able to do much. When his eyesight began to fail, he had to give up driving and poker—and, worst of all, reading. In early 1968 the cancer returned with a vengeance and he felt it in his heart that he would not beat it again. With that realization, he knew it was time, finally, to sit down and write that long-overdue letter to his son. He had put off the actual writing, but he had been making notes of what to say, and he had kept all those notes in his copy of *Self-Reliance*. There was a scrap of notebook paper here and a bit of torn-off newspaper there plus an envelope or two where he had jotted down things he wanted to be sure to include.

Finally one morning, he got an extra cup of coffee and sat down at his small study table with all his notes, and began to write. He figured he could leave the letter with his attorney and ask him to see that Frank received it after he was gone.

Clint died alone at the veterans' hospital in December 1968. By then, the cancer had spread to his heart and brain. On his small bedside table were four books with torn covers from significant use. Two of these lauded the wild Nebraska plains that Clint had loved so well: *Old Jules* by Mari Sandoz and *My Ántonia* by Willa Cather. The third was a book of poetry by Robert Burns, which he kept to remember his friend Duncan Laird, and the last, the thinnest and most battered of them all, was *Self-Reliance* by Ralph Waldo Emerson.

Who will tell whether one happy moment of love
or the joy of breathing
or walking on a bright morning and smelling the fresh air,
is not worth all the suffering and effort which life implies
— Erich Fromm

EPILOGUE
FATHER AND SON FIND PEACE

A Monday morning in October 1988, I was in my office preparing to leave for a flight to Washington, DC. My secretary stopped me just as I was leaving for the airport and said, "Mr. Morgan, there's a large envelope that just came in for you. Take it with you to look at during the flight."

I put it into my briefcase, which was already full with work I intended to do on the flight. All I was thinking about was that I was late; I had to get to the airport. My driver was waiting for me.

Once settled on the plane, I opened the envelope. On top of a large sealed packet were two letters, the first of which was from a Pender, Nebraska, attorney. His letter read:

Dear Mr. Morgan:

I obtained information on your whereabouts through your high school alumni association, and found what I believe to be your current address through local newspaper contacts. For some weeks now, since taking over files of my father's law practice, I have been trying to locate you because I came across a letter that should have been forwarded to you twenty years ago, in December 1968, at the time my father was settling your father's estate.

I feel certain that my father made every attempt to track your address in 1968 but was unable to get the enclosed into your hands. I thought you should have this now.

I looked again at the top of the letter, reading the name of the law firm in Pender, Nebraska, but barely glanced at the attorney's signature because I knew that what was enclosed must have come from my father's hand. I automatically calculated how many years had passed since I had seen him. Now a flash of emotion clearly identifiable as ancient anger tightened my chest, so I took a moment to compose myself before turning to the enclosure.

He had written the letter in 1968, twenty-two years after that moment at the rural highway where he had left me without a word or a look back. And from the time my father wrote the letter, another twenty years had now passed. I pulled up the tray beside my seat to provide a steady surface and laid the letter upon it.

November 11, 1968

Dear Son,

The editor of our newspaper told me you are now publisher of your own newspaper. Looks like you are finally going to make something of yourself.

Faint praise, I thought to myself. *That's my father, all right.*

As I come to the end of my life, it is my hope you can find a place in your heart to forgive me, as I do regret now that I haven't been able to bring myself to see you in all these years.

Well, your regret might be too little, too late.

There is something I should have told you years ago. My son, you have a sister you've never heard of before.

I have another sister? Oh my, a sister!

Her mother was Marie Mahoney. Remember that day in September 1936 when we were driving home from the Indian agency and stopped at her home for lunch? I hadn't seen her since 1917.

Boy, do I remember! When we got home, Mother was so angry. I was telling her about our afternoon with this nice lady, and she got so upset!

Many years ago, Marie and I were together at Careyhurst. She was with me before I left for France in May 1917. She was to stay at Careyhurst until I returned from World War I, but she didn't do that. The baby was born in February 1918 and was named Marie, for her mother. Now, Son, I didn't know about the child until 1955 when I learned about her from the family that raised her. Anyway, Marie didn't wait for my return from the war, and she didn't keep the baby with her either. Instead, she gave the child to my friend Frank McDuffie and his wife, who were neighboring ranchers near Careyhurst, and they adopted her and raised her as their own.

Your sister, Marie, is fifty years old now. She has made her life in Glenrock, married to the vice president of the bank there. I met her in 1955. She was a young woman of thirty-seven years of age then, and I told her about you and that someday I would make sure that the two of you got to meet each other.

So, Son, that brings me to the point of my writing to you now. I hope this letter reaches you.

Marie and I had much to remember in our relationship, which was symbolized for us by a lantern. It was special to us. When I collected Marie's ashes from the mortuary in Sioux City in 1955, I put her ashes inside that lantern and took it to Careyhurst—well, what used to be Careyhurst. The ranch had been sold in 1940 and was owned in 1955 by an insurance company. It had been renamed Bixby Ranch. But I went there and met with the manager of the ranch, a young fella by the name of John Martinez. I explained things to him and got his permission to take the lantern up into the hills adjacent to the ranch property, to government range land overlooking the Platte River Valley. I found a spot to bury the lantern with the ashes inside, and Martinez helped with the burial. Then I built a rock cairn over it.

Now, Son, there's something I want you and your sister to do for me.

Sure, you think you can ask a favor of me!

I know you might not think I have a right to ask anything from you, but I'm asking anyway. And it's not just for me, but for your sister and her mother and even for you yourself, in a way.

Now, there should be a package with this letter. Marie's friend Lily Lupino sent me these items a few years ago. They are keepsakes Marie had, and that's how I got them.

Wait a minute. Lily Lupino—I remember that name. I think I was maybe thirteen, in my first year of high school, when a traveling carnival set up on Main Street. I walked by one of the sideshows, then went behind and crawled under the tent to see what was going on inside. It was one of the worst geek shows I ever saw: a caged woman in a gunnysack biting the head off a chicken. I didn't want to see it but couldn't quit looking. Then a woman came up to me and asked me, "What are you doing here?" Right away she took me out the back of the tent. Outside, she looked closer at me and said, "Tell me, what is your name, young man?" I told her. She said, "I'm Lily Lupino, and I think I know your father. He's a fine man. Listen, you shouldn't be hanging around here. You be on your way now."

I want you and your sister to go together to see the manager of the Bixby Ranch. I don't know if John Martinez will still be there, but he'd be the best bet to help you find the burial site. When you dig it up, you'll find a pine box containing a lantern. I want you to add the contents of the package to the ashes in the lantern.

I guess that's all I have to say, Son.

— Clint Morgan

Well, I read that letter over and over, pretty much for the rest of the flight to DC. A nice meal was delivered to my first-class seat, but I wasn't interested in eating any of it. I asked the flight attendant to take it away. All I could think about was that forty-two years after his rejection of me, an amount of time that accounts for a lifetime of work by most standards, I finally heard from my father—and he had by that time been dead for twenty years!

Through all the years since that last silent parting between my father and me in 1946 in rural Nebraska, people have, from time to time, asked me about him. My usual response has been to brush off the questions and discourage the interest. I created a life for myself, a quite good life, and he was not a part of it. I chose university degrees and a life in the world of publication, knowing that farming—his vision for me—would never have been to my liking. Eventually I grew to accept the estrangement between us.

Now, I sat looking out the small plane window and wondering if I was glad to receive the letter or if things would have been better if we had just stayed estranged and I'd never heard from him again.

Then, as I thought over those forty-two years, I realized there was a time in my life when he might actually have been a little bit proud of me. In the 1970s, I was in the entertainment business, along with my newspaper career, and I was a producer of boxing events, including some major ones like the bouts of Ken Norton and Muhammad Ali. I was never myself the boxing champ my father was, but those fights I produced were the very kind of thing he would have appreciated.

By the time the flight landed and I had made my way by taxi to my hotel, I had settled down enough to have formed a plan. I called my secretary: "Louise, there are a couple of things I want you to do for me. First, see if you can find an address and phone number for a woman in Glenrock, Wyoming. All I can give you to go on is her first name is Marie, and her maiden name would have been McDuffie. She married a bank vice president. There aren't too many banks in Glenrock, so it

155

shouldn't be impossible. She'd be an older woman now, about sixty-nine or seventy years old, so her husband is likely retired."

Louise sounded dubious, but willing. "Okay, Mr. Morgan. I'll give it my best shot."

"I know you will. Then next, I want you to track down the manager of a ranch in Converse County, Wyoming. Years ago the ranch was called Careyhurst but it has different owners now, likely an insurance company, and it might be called Bixby Ranch. See if you can find a way to contact the current manager. Twenty years ago the ranch manager was a guy named John Martinez. We might get lucky and find that he's still around. He's really the man I need to see, if we can find him."

As I talked further with Louise, I realized that it would be helpful if she went ahead and made contact, if she could, with both Marie and John Martinez. It would save time if she could set appointments for me. "I'm changing my return flight to go to Cheyenne," I told Louise. "See if you can arrange for me to meet with Marie on Thursday, and then with Martinez on Friday."

By the time I reached Cheyenne and rented a car and driver, Louise had a phone number for me for Marie. I called Marie from the restaurant where we stopped for lunch. By now I was pretty well adjusted to the idea of having a sister, so I barged right in: "Marie, I expect you've heard my name by now. This is Frank Morgan. You and I shared a father, though it sounds like neither one of us spent a lot of time with him."

The small laugh that came over the phone line was uncertain and a little hesitant. When I heard her voice, I thought: *my goodness, this is my sister, and the first time I hear her voice, it's the voice of a grown woman no longer young.* "Yes," she said. "I—I've been expecting your call. Your father told me about you many years ago. I would like to have you come to see me."

"Well, I'm on my way to Glenrock now," I told her.

We met at the Hotel Higgins in Glenrock. I registered there, and then Marie came into the lobby. The resemblance to my father was faint, but it was there, and she didn't look as old as I had conjured in my mind. She seemed fit and strong, and crossed the lobby toward the desk with unexpected determination.

"I expect you're here to see me," I said, coming up to her at the desk before the clerk had asked if he could help her. She turned to me with clear, sharp eyes. I took her hand and held it maybe a moment longer than I would have the hand of any other complete stranger. Then we went to the dining room.

She was gracious, if not much of a talker, and she apologized more than once for staring at me as I explained about the letter and what I knew of what we were being asked to do. "It's really hard to believe, isn't it, our story? But I can see a bit of your father in you; I might call it a more refined version of your father."

That pleased me, I have to admit. But I was glad to move the conversation on to the task ahead of us. "I was able to talk to the ranch manager just before meeting you here," I told her. "My secretary tracked him down, and it turns out that he does remember Clint Morgan and the burial site there. 'Don't get that kind of request every day, ya know'—that's what he said." I smiled and so did she.

"It's remarkable you could find the man who knows where the lantern is buried," said Marie. "That is a vast, remote area out there."

"He said he'll have a pickup truck and a man and the tools we'll need ready to go tomorrow."

The next morning, I was at Marie's home early and drove the two of us to Bixby Ranch. Near the entrance to the large ranch an oversized black pickup truck was waiting. An older man emerged from the cab as we approached. "I'm John

Martinez," he said, taking off his right heavy-leather work glove to shake my hand. He nodded politely to Marie. He said he'd just been up to the burial site to make sure he could find it. Then he drove us into the hills. Amid tall grass, we found the rock cairn.

Despite his years, Martinez was agile and strong, and wasted no time piling the rocks to one side and digging down to the pine box. He had every tool he needed, including the pry bar to open the nailed box. Marie and I stood looking down into the grave as he took off the top. There was the lantern. It was larger than I had been expecting.

"Well, Marie," I said. "Why don't you go ahead and open that package and let's see what we're supposed to put inside this lantern." Meanwhile I knelt to lift the lantern, now rusted, out of the box. The weight of it shifted when I turned it upright, and I remembered that it was already full of ashes.

"These things, kept all these years," Marie said. One by one, she held them up to show me. One was a letter from France and a booklet that held The Lucky Gold Angel, a 20-franc gold coin. There was an envelope with a lock of Marie's hair, and another with a lock of Clint's hair. There were two train ticket stubs from a rail trip to Sioux City in 1912. There was a folded, weathered playbill of a vaudeville show at Dodge City featuring Marie and the von Essen brothers. Finally there was an envelope with a letter from Marie with the note: "Never to be opened."

With only a little force, I managed to overcome the rusted hinges to open the lantern, and she placed each item inside. The ranch manager stood a way off to one side to give us the time and privacy we needed. When we were finished and I had returned the now-heavy lantern to the pine box, he came back and efficiently returned the soil to the grave, then the rock cairn on top. Except for the grass that no longer stood tall and a little loose dirt, the site appeared undisturbed.

Strangely, neither Marie nor I was in any hurry to leave, and I guess Martinez noticed. He pointed off to his left and said, "I'm going to go check on some fence line just over this ridge. You two take the time you need. I'll come back later."

My sister and I sat down on a large rock that gave us a lookout over the meadow and across the valley of the North Platte River. No question, Clint had chosen a wonderful spot for the final resting place of the woman he had loved all his life, quite separate and apart from his feelings for my mother. Marie pointed to the wild roses I had not noticed amid the tall grass. In the distance I could just barely see the horns of a pronghorn antelope moving through the grass toward the river. I suddenly realized that the grass was the bluestem variety that my father had always spoken so highly of when I was a child.

Another memory of my father came to mind then. How often as a kid I had seen my father with his books, and the one that I thought of now was *My Ántonia*. There was a passage that he had underlined, and the page itself showed signs that he had returned to it again and again. I hadn't realized that it had lodged in my mind. As I breathed in deeply of the sweet breeze, I said to my sister, "Marie, this scene right here, it reminds me of that line Dad liked so much in *My Ántonia*: "…that is happiness; to be dissolved into something complete and great." I saw her nod so I went on. "Maybe that's the secret behind the devotion our father felt toward your mother, the very thing the lantern symbolized for the two of them all those years."

"It was several decades, really, that they loved each other," she said.

"Yes."

Then we were silent for some time. The longer we sat there, taking in the view and feeling the serenity that wafted up from the valley, the more my father's memory resolved itself inside me.

Finally, I could hear footsteps approaching and I knew Martinez was coming back. "Marie, we should go now," I said. She nodded.

As the big black pickup neared the entrance to the ranch, I took out my wallet and handed Martinez a hundred-dollar bill. He protested but I insisted, "No, I really want you to have it. You have been so helpful and so respectful how you went about it, so this is thanks for that."

Just before we got out of the truck, I added, "I'd like to think that you will, from time to time, make sure the burial site is undisturbed and that you'll keep it in your confidence that it is there."

"You can be sure I will," he said. I could see that he understood how important this was to my father and my sister and me.

On the drive back to Glenrock, Marie and I talked about our lives. I had already learned that she was a widow now, and even though her husband had left her well provided for, she still added to her income by giving piano lessons, and even played once in a while in the bar at the Hotel Higgins. Apparently, she had inherited some of her mother's flair for performance and entertainment.

We promised each other that we would stay in touch and make every effort to get together now and then. I bent down to kiss her cheek as I left her at her home, and she held me in her arms in a long embrace. Then we parted, and I motioned to my driver that I was ready to go.

We never saw each other again.

ABOUT THE AUTHOR

The setting of Frank H. Newell's childhood was Winnebago Indian land and a homestead farm in remote Nebraska during the Depression era of the 1930s. After graduation from high school, he enlisted in 1943 in the Army Air Corps, serving as a radio operator and aerial photographer in a 7th Air Force B-24. On August 9, 1945, he photographed the Nagasaki  devastation an hour after the detonation of the atom bomb. Following World War II, he earned a degree in journalism from Willamette University, Salem, Oregon, and worked fifty-eight years in the newspaper, entertainment, and broadcast businesses, including publishing, editorial and op-ed, and managing radio stations. In 2000 he was named Publisher of the Year by Wick Communications Company, owner of forty-four daily and weekly newspapers. After retiring at the age of 79, he continued to work as a consultant in media management. Today, he funds the annual Frank Newell Creative Writing Prize at Willamette University, and, at the age of 93, he is planning his next writing project. He and his partner, Marilyn Evans, live in Bellevue, Washington, and spend the winter months in Kauai, Hawaii.

Made in the USA
Coppell, TX
25 November 2021

66375586R00094